# CHRISTMAS CAROLS AND CANINE CAPERS!

A HOWLING GOOD CHRISTMAS MYSTERY!

THE TAMSIN KERNICK COZY ENGLISH MYSTERIES
BOOK 7

LUCY EMBLEM

This a work of fiction. Names, characters, places, buildings, businesses, products, and incidents are the product of the author's imagination. They bear no relation to actual persons, living or murdered, and every relation to The Malvern Hills, a designated National Landscape in the heart of England. The place is real, but the characters in this book are not, nor are many of the villages you'll visit.

Copyright © 2024 by Beverley Courtney Ltd

All rights reserved.

No portion of this book may be reproduced in any form without written permission from the publisher or author, except for the use of quotations in a book review.

First Edition 2024

## ALSO BY LUCY EMBLEM

More mysteries with Quiz, Banjo, and Moonbeam

Where it all began ..

Sit, Stay, Murder!

Ready, Aim, Woof!

Down Dog!

Barks, Bikes, and Bodies!

Ma-ah, Ma-ah, Murder!

Snapped and Framed!

Christmas Carols and Canine Capers! A Howling Good Christmas Mystery!

Game, Set, and Catch!

# CHAPTER ONE

"Not more decorations, Emerald?" Tamsin frowned as she tucked her unruly dark hair behind her ear, licked her fingers, and tried - cross-eyed - to thread her needle again.

"More. And more. And even more! I intend to fill up the whole house with them!" Tamsin's house-mate waved her long arms expansively, to encompass their home on Pippin Lane, nestled beneath the towering Malvern Hills which were visible from their back windows, and right now looking cold and dark in the December gloom.

"You really like Christmas, don't you."

Tossing her long ash-blonde hair back over her shoulder, Emerald stepped down from the chair. "I absolutely *love* it!" She waved her arm at the paper chains and tinsel she'd been pinning up across the ceiling. "It's so magical," she said dreamily, "I've always loved it. I love all the Christmas traditions. It makes me feel warm and cosy and .. safe."

"Warm and cosy and safe - all good," Tamsin conceded. "But you should feel pretty safe here with all these guardians," and she indicated her border collies Quiz and Banjo, lying on their beds watching Emerald's antics, a look of puzzlement on their faces.

"Hang on, where's Moonbeam?" She held up her hand and

listened. "Uh-oh, I hear paper tearing ..." Casting aside her sewing, she ran into the living room to find her little black and tan terrier Moonbeam busily dismembering a cardboard Father Christmas.

"Thank you, Moonbeam," the gentle dog trainer held out her hand and retrieved the shredded Santa, then grabbed a soft toy from the floor and tossed it to her little dog, exchange being no robbery. "I'm sorry Em! Have you got some tape? I'll mend it for you."

"Oh, don't worry, I have others. I'd better put the box of decorations up on the table to remove temptation." And as she bent to pick it up, said, "Opal! You're squashing everything!"

Tamsin laughed as she watched her housemate lift her big bushy cream cat out of the box, removing some tinsel from the long wispy hair behind her ears. "Well, we're even now!"

Emerald gave her cat a hug and a kiss before depositing her onto a dog bed next to Quiz, who sighed and put her chin on her paws, making room for the cat to curl up beside her, the cream of the cat's coat standing out against the black and sable collie coat. "But really, you don't like Christmas?"

"Not mad about it, no," Tamsin shrugged. "Although it's good to follow the ancient tradition and take time off in the middle of winter. I don't mind all that - and I'll definitely enjoy our carol-singing on Sunday! It's all the hype and madness for two months beforehand that gets my goat."

"Talking of goats," laughed Emerald, "we've been invited to visit Susannah's farm over Christmas!"

"Oh lovely! I haven't seen her for a while."

"She's up to her ears kidding at the moment."

"Kidding? At this time of year?"

"Yes, she's organising winter milk for her customers. She said she'll let us know when we can come."

"We'll definitely need to get our injection of kiddy fun and games! Banjo can come - he loves playing with those kids on their barrels and logs."

"And talking of fun and games, how's Banjo's Search & Rescue training going? You up the Hills this week?"

"No, we've finished till the New Year - apart from any call-outs for lost and wandering hikers with broken ankles. I'm really enjoying it! Banjo's doing fine with his cadaver scent training too."

Emerald shuddered at the mention of searching for dead bodies. "Thank goodness you haven't been called out for real yet - to search for a body, I mean."

"Not much call for it this weather," Tamsin joked. "People are too busy filling their larders and arguing over what sauce to serve with the turkey to be killing themselves - or each other!"

Emerald sat on the edge of Quiz's bed, her long legs crossed beneath her, and started making another paper chain. "It's a shame Christmas is so commercialised, I'd agree with you there. But it's good to have an excuse to do something different. You know," she added animatedly, as she hesitated to pick out a red paper strip, "for my last yoga class of the year I've asked everyone to wear something red or green. And I have some spicy candles to burn so that the room smells of Christmas."

"Sounds fun! And I have to admit I'm really looking forward to the fancy dress party for *my* last class of the year. There should be a great crowd, from all my different class venues."

They worked silently for a while, till Emerald had finished pinning up the latest batch of Christmas cards round the big mirror over the dining table and came over to look at what Tamsin was sewing. "Whose costume is that?"

"It's the apron for Moonbeam. She's going as Mrs. Mop. She's been learning to grip the dish-mop in her teeth."

"And what's this?" Emerald grinned as she dangled a headscarf with hair-rollers attached to it.

"That's her headscarf, covering her hair rollers! Used to be the traditional image of a cleaning lady, the flowered apron and headscarf knotted on top of her head, with her hair in rollers all day. But it's probably hopelessly out of date. The children will have no idea what she is.

I expect cleaning ladies these days wear trackie bottoms and earphones for their muzak."

"And manage all their bookings on their smartphones. But Charity will certainly recognise it."

"That'll do for me!" Tamsin smiled as she thought of their elderly friend, reminiscent of a busy little sparrow, who belied her age with her endless curiosity and energy.

"And what are the others going as? I've been so busy preparing red and green decorations for my class that I haven't caught up with you."

"Banjo is going as a pirate. Another knotted headscarf for him, but this time with these gold hoop earrings sewn on to it." She pointed out the blue scarf with its gold appendages. "He'll be gripping a knife in his teeth - cardboard covered in tin foil," she added quickly, seeing Emerald's look of dismay.

"And Quiz?"

"She's going as a 'sheep-dog'! I'm attaching the lambskin from beside my bed to her harness, so she can look like a sheep."

"Love it! Though I don't think I've ever seen a sheep with one ear up and one ear down," Emerald laughed gaily. "May I come?"

"Oh, absolutely! I could really do with another pair of hands. I'm sure there'll be some dogs with 'wardrobe malfunctions' who could do with a bit of help. And you'll know quite a few of the students anyway. It's being held at Nether Trotley Village Hall, but all my students are invited. We had a big turn-out last year - lots from Malvern, and some came over from the Hereford classes."

"And that's what you were shopping for last week? All the prizes?"

"Yep. Gotta have prizes!"

"And how many will *you* win?"

"None!" Tamsin fastened off her sewing and snapped the thread. "I'm just joining in to encourage the others. And I went shopping for little cakes too, of course."

"No mince pies?"

Tamsin lowered her sewing and looked sternly at her friend. "Now,

Emerald, you know the house rules about mince pies. I don't want any dogs spending Christmas in intensive care at the vet's."

"Oh yes, I do remember. Yes. Sorry! No mince pies in this house."

"Or Christmas cake either - just as deadly for dogs."

"The raisins, right?"

"The raisins. But fortunately we *are* allowed to eat them when we're out of the house!"

"What would Christmas be without mince pies? Have you seen the posh ones at The Cake Stop?"

"I'm afraid I've already sampled a goodly number of them. This year the Furies have featured lots of flaked almonds on the top. They're quite delicious."

"And masses of icing sugar all over them! So we've found something you *do* like about Christmas!"

"Yeah. I'm not a complete Scrooge," Tamsin grinned. "Don't worry Em, I'll soften as the day gets closer." She sighed and pushed all her costumes into a large bag. "But right now, it's *walk time!*" She smiled as the dogs all leapt from their beds as if catapulted, and in the flurry of waving tails and excited yips from the little terrier, she pulled on her thick coat and boots and got the dogs dressed in their leads and harnesses, and a woollen coat for thin-skinned Moonbeam. "I have to walk off some of these mince pies!"

"Oh yeah, It'll be dark by four, I keep forgetting. I do hate these gloomy days," Emerald pulled a face.

"Not long till the longest night - then we'll start gaining back a minute or so a day." Tamsin pulled her woolly hat firmly down over her ears as she opened the back door.

"And I for one, can't wait!"

## CHAPTER TWO

Munching yet more luxury almond mince pies was just what Tamsin found herself doing at her favourite coffee shop in Great Malvern the next day, along with Charity Cleveland and her motley crew of carol-singers. A last-minute meeting had been called to nail down the details for Sunday night. The town was busy as people prepared for Christmas, decorations sparkling in all the shop windows. Near the cheap fashion shops, the teenagers gathered as usual in small groups, affecting nonchalance and scorn for tradition. But Tamsin knew well that those same teenagers would be eagerly ripping open their presents on the big day.

"You are building up your energy for your singing, *n'est-ce pas?*" asked Jean-Philippe as, tea-towel over his shoulder as always, he cleared some of the mugs and empty plates.

"Absolutely! And these mince pies are gorgeous - the Three Furies have excelled themselves," Tamsin nodded to Electra - who surprisingly, as the shyest of the three sisters who made up Dodds & Co, providers of mouthwatering cakes to The Cake Stop - had decided to add her voice to the choir. Electra blushed and fluttered.

Tamsin was always amused when she or anyone else used the

Furies' nickname - which referred to the fact that the three sisters each had a name from Greek mythology, thanks to their Ancient-Greece-obsessed mother. They were three remarkable and very different sisters, of which Electra was the middle one, and definitely the most diffident.

Charity made a slight cough to call the group to order. "So we all know what we're doing now?" asked the diminutive old lady, perched erect on her chair, her fluffy brown dog Muffin contentedly lying on a mat at her feet with Tamsin's little black and tan terrier Moonbeam.

Most of the assembled singers nodded.

Except for Dorothy, whose elderly voice trembled as she waved her hand nervously. "I'm sorry, I've forgotten which carol we're starting with."

"*God rest ye merry gentlemen*," Shirley Vaughan, who'd been making notes, was quick to give her the answer. "A nice rousing one to get us warmed up."

"I think we'll *need* warming up if it stays this cold!" said Shirley's son Mark Bendick, who'd been roped in because of the eternal shortage of men singers.

"We can walk briskly to the first house," suggested plump Hilda, who had been hugely enjoying eating a delicious treat that for once she hadn't baked herself in her own commercial kitchen at *Hilda's Homebakes*. And accordingly she'd already devoured two of the large mince pies.

"I think we'll have to walk briskly to keep up with Cameron and Alex and Joe!" laughed Molly, thinking of her three boys. "They're so excited, it's not true. The teachers have been bribing them to behave for months now, under threat of Santa passing our chimney over."

"That's mean!" piped up one of the older singers. "It's nice that they're excited. I so love Christmas - and when I was a child it was so special. Those teachers should enjoy their childish enthusiasm!"

"They complain enough about children behaving like louts," Shirley sucked her teeth with disdain. "They should encourage them at this time of year."

There were some nods and mumbles of agreement. Colonel Simkins' deep voice (he was a pillar of the bass line) could be heard gruffly agreeing about the solemnity and importance of the season and the behaviour of the children, "Mind you, they may be excited, but the school still needs to keep order."

Shirley was nibbling the end of her pen as she frowned at her notebook. "So we're starting off at seven o'clock in Avenue Road, then heading down to Barnard's Green ..."

"That's right, dear, Sunday at seven." said Charity. "Then along Poolbrook, a couple of carols at The Goat and Compasses, up past the Chase School and the Science Park, and we have to be back at the Churchwarden's house by half past eight. He's so excited, and he always gives us a great spread of food and mulled wine to warm us and help us on our way home."

"That's quite an expedition! We'll need the food and wine by then," laughed Shirley.

"I was talking to Peter Threlgood the other day," said Dorothy, feeling more sure of herself now, but with a blush she quickly added, "I saw him in the Post Office." She coughed. "He sees our carol singing as a high point of his Christmas! He's really looking forward to the evening."

"Dear old chap," agreed Tamsin. "And he adores that dog of his, Toffee. He's been on a few of my *Top Dogs* walks. Oh, are we bringing dogs, Charity?"

"Absolutely! As long as it's not raining. Muffin hates the rain, don't you Muffie-puff?"

"What about you, dear? Who will you bring?" asked Hilda the baker, who'd got to know Tamsin and her dogs over the contamination scare in the Farmers' Market. She shifted her plentiful bulk heavily in her chair to look round at her.

"Quiz will enjoy it. But Banjo wouldn't - too shy. And Moonbeam wouldn't like standing around in the cold listening to me caterwauling!"

"Doesn't she have a warm coat?" asked Shirley, looking at the tiny dog curled up with Muffin.

Tamsin felt slightly aggrieved that there hadn't been a universal denial from everyone that her singing could be described as 'caterwauling', but she felt that served her right for fishing, and let it pass. "She has a lovely peach-coloured coat that Charity knitted for her, embroidered with moonbeams. But she still wouldn't appreciate standing still in the cold for long. Look at those spindly legs!" She nodded to the bed where Moonbeam was snuggled up in Muffin's fluff.

"They look even tinier to me!" laughed Shirley, "after looking at Luke's tree-trunk legs all day. I think I'll bring him. He doesn't mind the cold at all."

"Being a Pyrenean Mountain Dog has its advantages at this time of year," agreed Tamsin.

"So there'll be nineteen of us altogether," with a flourish of the pen Shirley drew a line under the list of names in her book, "plus a few children."

"And at least three dogs!" said Tamsin with a grin.

Charity was frowning, still trying to get things organised. "I'll give you all the carol books when we meet up - they're heavy, so I'll have them in a box in the boot of my car. Do take care of them, won't you all? They're ever so expensive."

"We will," chirruped a few voices.

"And if you can get Chas to join us, Molly, that would be wonderful!" Charity went on. "It's so hard to get men to take part. We're very fortunate in having Colonel Simkins," the named gentleman pulled back his shoulders and sat to attention with a deep 'harrumph', "and Mark is a great addition this year." Mark was busy staring at his phone till his mother elbowed him and he waved a hand in acknowledgement of the compliment.

"Actually," he said, coming to attention, "there's a friend of mine who may like to come. I know he sings very loud at football matches!" Shirley beamed at her son as Hilda and Charity exchanged rueful glances.

"We'll have to bring the baby too, if Chas comes," said Molly. "So if it's decent weather, he'll be there."

"How old is she now, dear?" asked Hilda.

"Just over one!"

"An enchanting age," coo-ed Dorothy. She turned to Tamsin, "Will your young man be there, dear, to write something for the paper?"

"Feargal? He's not my young man, Dorothy - sorry to disappoint you! And he won't be coming - he's in the Alps on a skiing holiday. But you could always send some photos direct to the *Malvern Mercury*. One of his colleagues there will help you, I'm sure."

"That's a good idea! Now, I wonder who will take the photos …" and spotting Mark fiddling with his phone again, she invited him. He couldn't really wriggle out of it, so he agreed, his mother smiling proudly beside him.

Then the happy band all fell to chattering about their Christmas shopping, the best way to roast potatoes, where to find holly, the magic ingredient for mince pie pastry - Hilda insisted the secret was lime zest, at which Electra nodded sagely - and other such important details for the season. The two elderly ladies from the Women's Institute were particularly vocal on the subject of Christmas Pudding.

"And where will you be on The Day, Tamsin?" asked Dorothy.

"Ah, I'll be visiting my Mum in Brum. My brother will be there too, with his wife and three kids. So it'll be noisy!"

"Birmingham is always noisy," said Electra, passing a hand over her brow. Even the thought of noise was too much for her. "And dear Emerald?"

"She's off to join her wacky mother on her houseboat for a couple of days."

"Oh, I'm so glad you won't be alone for the day," said Dorothy. "No-one should be alone at Christmas, I always think. Peter has invited me round to his for Christmas lunch. So thoughtful of him." She blushed again and her old cheeks dimpled. "I made sure not to take any B&B bookings over the Christmas period, so I'll be able to do some baking to take with me on the day."

"I'm sure you'll have a lovely time," Tamsin smiled, thinking of all the duty invitations and visits being planned round the country over the festive season. She loved her family and got on fine with them, as long as they kept a respectful distance from each other for most of the year, but she really was happiest at home in Pippin Lane with her 'family' of dogs and her very own dog training business. And once the fancy dress party and the carol-singing were done she was looking forward to plenty of peace and quiet over the Christmas break to enjoy long walks along the Malvern Hills with her dogs, before classes started up again in January.

Sugarloaf Hill, Pinnacle Hill, Midsummer Hill, Hangman's Hill, Broad Down, Raggedstone Hill, and so many more: their names rolled round her mouth like fine wine. And she thought of the great expanses of sheep-cropped grass on the bare summits. She'd heard that the very name Malvern came from the ancient British *moel-bryn,* meaning a bare hill. She so enjoyed sharing these windswept hills with her dogs, the occasional walkers, and the wheeling buzzards overhead, plaintively mewing as they circled. Her mind wandered off from the busy café into a reverie of invigorating walks she'd enjoyed in the past ...

How soon was her longed-for peace and solitude to be shattered!

# CHAPTER THREE

"We need a break!" Emerald got the mugs ready and flipped on the kettle.

Tamsin looked up from her laptop. "Can't wait! I had more classes than ever this year. I'm setting up another Hereford class starting in February, and my new home training packages are getting a great take-up. I *definitely* need a break!" She leant back in her chair and stretched her arms up over her head. "Aaahh. All those leisurely tramps over the Hills. And I'll start tomorrow, with Midsummer Hill."

"You don't mind Midsummer after .. you know .. what happened up there?"

"Not me! People have walked these Hills for millennia. That was just a blip. I'll exorcise any demons by enjoying walking the ancient earthworks of the fort."

"Wrap up warm! The North-East wind up there is biting."

"Keeping up with this crowd keeps me pretty warm," laughed Tamsin. "They can run up and down those Hills with no effort at all."

Emerald stared at the kettle for a moment, waiting for it to boil. "I've done my last class, so it's just tomorrow's carols to go."

"The carols are fun. Such a funny group of people Charity's gathered together."

"Where does she get them from? And how does she persuade them to join in?" Emerald languidly fiddled with the end of her long blonde plait.

"Goodness knows! Charity has an almanac for a brain. She knows everything about everybody."

"And their parents and grandparents, uncles and aunts ..."

"That too! Her extensive family knowledge has certainly helped us nail down an evil-doer on more than one occasion."

"Indeed," Emerald clattered some spoons as Opal wound her massive cream-furry self round her ankles. "Ok, ok, Opal. You've had breakfast ages ago." But she was still persuaded to dish out some more for the cat, who, in her defence, was shapely and agile as well as beautiful, just like her owner.

"She's a remarkable person. And such fun! Hey - talking of remarkable people, any news from Susannah yet?"

"Nope. It's a busy time for her. She told me once that she always knew when kids were going to be born that night. Something to do with feeling the mother's flanks every day. But she also said that she couldn't bear to miss out if she'd been wrong, and something bad happened. So she still gets up in the night regardless."

"That's Susannah alright! Belt and braces. She must be whacked." Tamsin turned back to her laptop and worked on her timetables for a few moments.

"The carols are taking a long route, from what you told me." Emerald put the steaming mugs of coffee down on the table.

"Thanks, Em! I've done enough planning. I've been at it all morning," Tamsin spoke with feeling. "I'll get back to it later .. after Christmas, with a bit of luck!" She snapped her laptop shut - a sound that caused the dogs to lift their heads and look hopefully at her, then sighed with disappointment as Tamsin wrapped her fingers round her mug. "Yes, we'll be in need of sustenance by the time we reach Threlgood's place. I believe Dorothy is helping with his food - he always gives us loads. Sausages, mince pies, mulled wine. It's really nice!"

"And who is he, exactly?" Emerald straightened the crepe paper ribbon the Christmas cards were pinned to and sat down at the table.

"He's an old boy. He was a surveyor for the Council, then when he retired he was elected as one of the Churchwardens."

"Charitable post, is it?"

"Oh no, he gets a salary. Must do quite well along with the pension he gets from the Council. He doesn't have any family as far as I know. No wife in evidence, anyway."

"So what does a Churchwarden actually do?"

"Probably exactly what I'm doing right now - planning! Planning out the year for the church. General assistant to the Rector, I guess. And, of course, being a surveyor, I understand he has the overview of the church's condition, structurally, you know?"

"So he's a pillar of society," Emerald's voice had a slightly mocking tone.

"Yes," laughed Tamsin. She knew her friend didn't have too high a regard for organised religion. "But he seems a decent soul. I think Dorothy's carrying a torch for him. She was telling me the other day what a wonderful person he is. But I think she may be barking up the wrong tree there. He appears to be a confirmed bachelor."

"And what does Charity say about him?"

"How perceptive you are, Emerald! When Dorothy was doing the 'everybody loves him' act, Charity was casting her eyes heavenward."

"So he's not as pure as the driven snow, after all."

"I don't think anyone who reaches that age has managed to make no enemies at all. I'm sure I've made loads already. You'd be a bit milk-and-water if you never managed to rub anyone up the wrong way."

"That's true, I suppose. I'd hate to think I've ever upset anyone." Emerald sighed as she gave a hug to Opal, now seated on her lap doing her post-prandial washing. "I'll have to see when we get there, and make up my own mind about him. I'm usually quite quick to sum people up."

"You are gifted in that way. So," Tamsin glanced out of the window and putting her mug down with a bang she stood up. "Two o'clock! I'm going to walk these three before it gets dark - still gets dark so early."

Quiz, Banjo, and Moonbeam were ecstatic - they had been right! The snap of the laptop shutting had presaged a walk. 'Clever dogs' their dancing bodies and waving tails were saying. And Tamsin joined in too, "Clever dogs!" she said as she gathered coats - one for Moonbeam and one for herself, leads, frisbees, treats, and all the paraphernalia needed for a good dog walk.

"You'll find out about Peter Threlgood tomorrow!" she said to Emerald as she disappeared out the back door.

## CHAPTER FOUR

It was a chilly and damp December evening on Sunday, and Tamsin had settled Banjo and Moonbeam and was leading up Quiz, ready for the Carol-singing.

"Know who I saw this morning on my walk?" Standing near the door and wrapping her scarf round her long neck, Emerald looked expectantly at her. "It was Dorothy. She'd just been delivering goodies to Peter for tonight."

"That's good news. By the time we get to his house we'll be cold and starving. And you tell me he puts on a good spread?"

"He does! I didn't realise till now that some of it comes from Dorothy. Clearly Charity has slipped up and not kept me abreast of every detail of every friendship in all of the Malverns!"

"Tut-tut," laughed Emerald as she pulled her gloves out of her pocket. "I'm looking forward to the carols too. I used to love singing at school, and apart from singing along to the radio I haven't done any since then."

"We'll soon blow away the cobwebs when we get going with *God rest ye merry gentlemen!*"

"As long as no-one can hear me making a squawky noise, I'm fine."

Tamsin laughed. "Hilda will be singing the solo in *Silent Night*. She's so brave! I'd never dare sing out loud on my own."

"She has hidden talents, then - along with all her baking at *Hilda's Homebakes*." Emerald pulled her big woolly hat down over her ears, threaded her fingers into her gloves, and announced herself ready. The three of them set off in the trusty *Top Dogs* van.

It was cold and blustery by the time the singers all met up in Avenue Road, but fortunately not raining. The bare trees were swaying slightly with the gusts, and a few leftover leaves and a stray chocolate wrapper swirled along the road before the wind slackened for a while to refresh itself for the next gust.

The boot of Charity's little blue car was open, revealing a couple of boxes of carol books for people to borrow. There was a book for each family so that the parents could hold them for the children to share - the books were awkward to handle as the wind blew the pages over if not firmly clamped by a strong hand. And a carol book landing upside down in an icy puddle was not a good idea!

As the choir all gradually assembled, there was much excitement, and also much stamping of feet and muffled clapping of gloved hands to try and warm up. Colonel Simkins, whose opportunities to give orders were severely limited since his retirement, was happily issuing instructions to Mark and the other men who'd arrived, as to who was to sing which bit. "I'll sing bass along with Chas and Kevin. You four can sing the tenor line there," his gruff voice announced to the whole group. Martin the chiropractor nodded, Steve the tobacconist wasn't listening but talking to his wife Dottie, while Mark looked totally nonplussed, having no idea which line was which. They didn't teach reading music in clink. His friend, who rejoiced in the name Manic, was clearly thinking of something else altogether as he gazed into the distance.

These orders were interrupted by shrieks of excitement as three boys in their red and green bobble hats cascaded along the pavement to join them, hotly followed by their mother, and more slowly by Chas with Amanda in her pushchair - almost invisible in her yellow hooded snowsuit and heaps of blankets, with a toy giraffe firmly grasped in her chubby hand to wave at people and use as a shillelagh.

"I think we're all here now Charity," said Shirley, with half an eye on her big friendly Luke who was being greeted and patted by Alex and Joe, whose nose was about level with Luke's. Cameron was keener to meet Quiz, who was a special friend of his - having rescued him from a serious scrape not so long ago - and he knew that a brief greeting was all she required.

Charity clapped her hands for attention. "It's wonderful that you can all be here tonight. We're going to have a wonderful time! I think you all have a book?"

"I haven't got a book!" wailed Joe.

"It's just for the grown-ups, silly," said Cameron, giving him a big sideways push. Chas took Joe's hand and steered him to the safe side of Amanda's pushchair, then put a soothing hand on his red and green woolly hat.

"And who'd like to carry these collecting buckets?"

"Me!" chorused three small boys.

"You can take turns, alright? Remember to hold the bucket with the label at the front, so people can see they're contributing to the church tower fund. I've put a bit of change in so they rattle." And she passed one bucket to Cameron, one to Colonel Simkins, and one to Mark. She had passed over Electra who was standing beside Mark, as Charity knew she'd never be bold enough to actually collect any money from anyone. "Now, we're going to walk down a little before we start." And she turned to set off down the hill, a very small Pied Piper with all the rats following her.

"How do we get our note?" asked Dorothy. "We do all want to start on the same note!"

"Oh. I'm not sure. Marjorie used to bring her recorder, but she couldn't be here this year. She's visiting her daughter's family in France for Christmas, you know. She's been looking forward to it for ages. You remember Marjorie's daughter Annette, Dorothy?" Dorothy frowned as she tried to remember Annette.

"Bet she's got it warmer than we have!" Mark started to jump up and down on the spot, which got Alex going and the two of them jumped together.

"I've got my phone with me," Tamsin volunteered. "I'm sure I can find a way of getting a note from that .. hang on a minute while I hunt." She whipped out her phone and started tapping on it. "Yes, here we go! I've found a virtual tuning fork."

"Whatever will they think of next?" asked Dorothy.

"I'll take the note from the carol book and this app will give me the sound. Can you all hear it?" She played an A on her phone and held it up in the air. A few of them hummed the note correctly, and rather more hummed some other note entirely.

"Oh thank you dear!" Charity said warmly. "I'd entirely forgotten about Marjorie's recorder. Let's begin here, near the vet's. We should catch a few people going in and out." They gathered on a wide section of pavement outside the vet clinic.

Kevin Prenderghast had a traditional-looking LED lantern which he'd fixed to a pole. "It was in my garden shed - thought it would be just the thing for today," he explained. Really, thought Tamsin, he looks like an eager boy scout.

"It's perfect!" said Charity. "Very festive - thank you, dear."

So Tamsin found the note for *God rest ye, merry gentlemen* and with a firm downbeat from Colonel Simkins - who was delighted to have found another way to organise people - they started off, gradually gaining confidence and beginning to sound pretty good in the cold night air. They bunched up closer to hear better in the wind, which was snatching their voices away. Cameron stood proudly holding out his bucket.

"You have to rattle it!" hissed Alex, and grabbed his brother's arm to shake the bucket about. And between them they made such a big rattling noise that Chas had to intervene to get them to quieten down a bit so that the singing wasn't drowned out.

Some of the vet nurses came out to enjoy the carol and put some money in the buckets. They gave a surprised wave to their nurse colleague Melanie, who was spending her evening off with the carollers. And with many heartfelt Christmas wishes, and flushed with their success, the group processed down the hill a bit further for their next carol.

They all got into the swing of it and were singing with gusto by the time they'd serenaded the Chinese takeaway and the burger place at Barnard's Green, where their filling buckets started to get heavy. Then singing at a few houses en route, they reached The Goat and Compasses on Poolbrook Common.

The boys, whose excitement was turning to tiredness, only squabbled a little, not wanting to show themselves up in front of the girls from their school who were also in the group. The girls stuck out their tongues to make their opinion of the boys clear, and keep them in their place.

Every now and then baby Amanda woke and brandished her giraffe at anyone who got close enough, with a loud "Ma-ma-ma-maahh!". And when they reached the pub they were invited in to sing in the saloon bar. The canned muzak was turned down for them, the children were invited to stand on benches, and the clanking of the buckets suggested that they were collecting a good sum.

"Here you go! Merry Christmas to you all!" said the rosy-cheeked landlord as he passed round some tiny mince pies with little pastry stars on. Joe put one in his mouth and one in his pocket, till his father tapped him on the shoulder with a slight shake of the head, so he pulled the now-fluffy pie from his pocket and crammed that one in his mouth too. The singers tucked in, delighted to get out of the wind for a while, and insisted on singing three carols, to make the most of it. By this stage the jolly landlord was not enjoying the sound of silence from his tills, and stepped forward with a brief speech of thanks and some hip-hip-hoorays to terminate the visit.

"Well, that's warmed me up!" said Hilda, who'd sung her verse of *Silent Night* very prettily - even getting a round of applause from the patrons - as they emerged once more onto the road and started to trudge up the hill in the dark, windy night, all happily chattering.

Tamsin was talking to the vet nurse Melanie, who seemed to think that her veterinary work was far more important than dog training, and that she was much superior to this doggy know-all. As soon as she was able, Tamsin moved off to more congenial company. She noticed Emerald in conversation with Kevin Prenderghast, the owner of the insurance business over the bookshop. She hadn't actually met him before, only heard him described mockingly as 'Old Prenderghast' by his receptionist. In fact, he was younger than she expected, and looked quite presentable, if rather stressed by life in general.

"Here Dad, can you carry this bucket? It's getting awfully heavy," Cameron and Alex were holding the bucket between them and were clearly getting tired. Chas took the bucket in one hand, holding Joe's hand in the other, as they walked past the school - deserted at this time of night.

"Is that Big School?" Alex asked excitedly, now able to hop about again, having been freed of his burden.

"That's right," said Molly, pushing the sleeping Amanda's chair, her giraffe clutched to her under the blankets. "Cameron will be starting there in a couple of years."

"Coo," said the awed Joe, as Alex danced away.

A minor squabble had broken out between the other children.

"There's *three* Malverns," said Alex emphatically, jumping in.

"No, there's not. There's four!" said his older brother.

"Name them, then," the younger of the two girls jutted her chin out.

"Um," said Alex slowly, "Great Malvern, Little Malvern .."

"Malvern Link!" interrupted Joe excitedly, waving his hands in the air with pride.

"And Malvern Wells. There. Four of them," said Cameron with finality, folding his arms in front of him.

"You're forgetting West Malvern - that's where my Granny lives," said the older girl, with a look of 'I told you so', though she hadn't actually offered a number of Malverns.

The boys sulked for a moment before dismissing the subject by racing ahead to catch up Mark to ask him about the latest cycling classes being run by *Flying Pedals,* the bike shop where he worked.

Looking up at the Hills rising above the town, the lights from houses glimmering along its sides, Emerald said, "I always think the Hills look like an ocean liner at night."

"Yes, you're right! The lights are in rows because the houses are on the top road - they do look like rows of cabin portholes!" agreed Shirley.

They passed the Science Park which had only a few security lights burning and wasn't considered worth a carol. Rather, they pressed on towards the promise of food at the party.

After singing outside a few more houses *en route,* with varying degrees of success, they all filed into the Churchwarden's front garden just as a fine drizzle began, and with a note from Tamsin's phone and a sign from Colonel Simkins, struck up *O Come All Ye Faithful*. Peter Threlgood appeared at the front door and smiled beatifically as they sang. And when they got to the last rousing chorus of *O come let us adore him,* holding the carol books close to them to avoid them getting wet, he applauded loudly, with cries of "Bravo!" and invited them all in.

"Come in carollers! Come in, out of the cold!" said Peter as they all filed past him. "You can park your books on the hall table while you eat."

There were many rosy faces as they admired the elegant room and gradually began to warm up round the blazing fire, able to open their jackets and peel off their gloves and hats. The children made short work of the sausage rolls and orange juice, and Cameron and Alex were delighted to meet another dog - Peter's Golden Retriever Toffee.

"The rain's let up a bit - would you like to play with Toffee in the garden?" asked their host. "He loves his ball."

So the three boys ran out whooping to the garden - Alex grabbing a handful of sugared almonds on the way and stuffing them in his pocket - and the room instantly became several degrees calmer. With a resigned look at each other, the two young girls followed them outside, their mother Sandra urging them on. Everyone remaining was happy to accept a glass of mulled wine and plough through the food on offer.

"I'm not sure about that friend of Mark's," Charity said very quietly to Tamsin. "Looks a bit of a wide boy."

"I hope Shirley's antennae are bristling then! I believe he's one of Mark's colleagues from his rehab course - the motorbike maintenance one. I'm not mad about all those tattoos and chains round his neck - looks quite alarming. And who disports himself in a sleeveless t-shirt at this time of year?

"That's to show off his muscles!"

"Of course! Who's that talking to Shirley now?"

"Oh that's Martin Bramwell. He's a chiropractor, or osteopath, or physio, or something. I never know the difference. Knows everyone's secrets, I expect!"

Colonel Simkins was busy lecturing Steve and Dottie, who ran the tobacconists down in Malvern Link. Backed up against the wall, they fiddled with their empty plates until Dottie plucked up the courage to go and re-fill hers.

The two ladies from the WI had found kindred souls in Hilda and Dorothy and were busily comparing notes on baking. Quiz lay on the rug in front of the fire with Muffin, clearing up the flaky crumbs from the sausage rolls they'd just been given. "They're having mine," Charity was assured by Emerald, who didn't eat meat. Luke looked like a big white hearth-rug as he quietly slumbered near them, his big chest rising and falling peacefully.

"They look tired," Emerald observed to Tamsin, getting nearer to the heat of the fire.

"I think they'll stay at least half-awake as long as the titbits keep coming!" laughed Tamsin. She glanced around the room. "It's a big house, this. I see people are wandering about from room to room."

"Apparently Peter has a large collection of watercolours in the dining room. Someone just told me. Want to have a look?"

"Yes, let's!" and they turned to head for the dining room.

That was the moment a scream pierced the party.

There was an instant hush in the room. Hilda dropped her plate onto the wooden floor with a crash. The chiropractor's face paled. Dottie clung to Steve's elbow. Molly instinctively scooped up Amanda from her pushchair and held her close. Chas ran to the back door he'd just come through, to check on his boys.

A white-faced Dorothy staggered out of the dining room, pointing soundlessly back into the room, before fainting into the capable arms of Mark who had jumped forward in the nick of time to catch her.

Colonel Simkins glanced into the room then took over. "All stay where you are!" he commanded. And everyone froze to the spot. "Bramwell, come with me."

They went into the room. Tamsin reached the doorway and peered in. Peter Threlgood was lying on the floor, collapsed in an awkward position, his face towards her. She put her hand to her face and looked desperately at Emerald. "It's happened again," she mouthed. "The Churchwarden is dead."

## CHAPTER FIVE

It's fair to say that chaos ensued. Dorothy came to, looked about her frantically, then went into hysterics. Melanie and Martin were dragooned into looking after her, being the only people there with any medical qualifications.

Colonel Simkins came into his own and issued orders with gusto. The first being to barricade the dining room entrance with two of the rather beautiful Queen Anne dining chairs, then to instruct Kevin Prenderghast to call the police and ambulance.

Emerald exuded calmness, getting Charity and Hilda to comfort the two WI ladies who were taking it all very badly.

"Such a lovely man!" wailed one.

"Always so kind!" replied her friend.

"He must have had a heart attack,' said Hilda. "He *was* getting on," she added quietly.

"He was not that old .." objected the very elderly Charity, who was at least ten years older than the defunct Churchwarden.

Tamsin took care of Toffee who was anxious to get into the room to see his master, and as she took him out to the kitchen to find one of his toys - determined to let the dog sniff Peter before the night was out -

she saw Electra emerging from the morning room which led off it. She was scurrying like a little mouse and wedging something deep into her cardigan pocket. When she saw Tamsin the other side of the kitchen island she blushed, then paled. Tamsin reckoned the best course of action was to say nothing. For now. But she had carefully logged this strange behaviour.

She returned to the living room to hear Colonel Simkins clearing his throat to make an announcement. "Everyone will have to stay here till the police have been. But I really think the families with children should go home."

This was greeted with general nods and murmurs of assent.

"Right," said Chas, who had three ashen-faced silent boys clinging to him. "You know where we are if they need to talk to us. But I was over by the front window with Molly and Amanda and Sandra, till I went out to the garden where the children were playing with Threlgood's dog. I'd just come back in when .. when .."

Sandra said, "Oh thank you, yes, we need to go home. I was talking to Molly a lot of the time. Isn't that right, Molly?" She reached out to clasp the hands of her two girls, one of whom was grizzling quietly.

Molly nodded and started to shepherd the children out. "Can we leave the books here, Charity?" she asked, as she manoeuvred the pushchair through the doorway.

"Oh yes, of course. Don't worry about them now, dear. I can collect them later." And as the two families left to hurry to their cars the sound of police sirens could be heard approaching.

The room transformed from a pleasant cosy party room to a crime scene, as the large police officers in their bulky kit took over. The paramedics were close behind with all their paraphernalia taking up half the room, the flashing lights from the emergency vehicles in front of the house casting a weird blue flickering light through the partly open curtains.

"I really think we ought to call the Rector," Charity was trying to get the attention of the police sergeant. "After all, Peter was the Churchwarden. Maybe the Rector should anoint him or something?"

"By all means give him a call. But the police and paramedics will need to examine him first." Charity scurried off to the hallway where the house phone was located, thumbing through the address book on the antique table to find the Rector's number.

Tamsin had parked Quiz and Toffee next to Muffin in front of the fire, to which Mark was adding some more coal. "We should at least keep warm," he muttered. Tamsin put a hand on his shoulder then sidled over to the dining room doorway to do a bit of eavesdropping.

The police and the medics had their heads together. "So you're not satisfied?" the police sergeant asked.

"No. Something weird here. It doesn't look like a heart attack. Sudden fatal collapse will need investigating."

"Ok. Then we'll need to get the Scene of Crime chaps over here to photograph everything before he's moved."

"Right. We'll leave you to it then. There'll be calls stacking up for people we *can* help," and with a wry smile the paramedics set about packing up their gear and headed out to their ambulance.

"Looks as though we'll be here for a while," Tamsin whispered to Emerald as she went back to the dogs. "They reckon it's an unnatural death."

"Oh Lord," sighed Emerald. "Why did I ever think Malvern was a peaceful place?"

"You know it's lovely - most of the time," Tamsin smiled. "While we wait to be interviewed, we should be fixing everything firmly in our mind - remembering exactly who, and what, and where."

"There was a lot of movement - people going out to the garden, going upstairs to the bathroom, plenty in and out of the dining room, the kitchen ..."

"Let's sit and think quietly. See what we can remember."

And they both sat down on the hearth rug with the dogs and thought.

The police commandeered the kitchen for their interviews, but Hilda rushed in first asking if she could make tea for everyone. "They really need it! They're in shock," she assured the sergeant.

"Ok. But be quick about it," he said.

So Hilda called Charity and Shirley in to speed things up - the two Women's Institute ladies were still collapsed in their armchairs twittering - as the sergeant cast his eyes up at his constable, who was grinning at him.

It wasn't long before the ladies carried a couple of trays into the living room, with teapot, milk and sugar on one, and many cups and saucers on the other. Hilda offered the policemen a cup. The Sergeant hesitated for a moment then said, "Go on then," but he declined any of the food. "Could you ask people to come in one at a time please?"

Colonel Simkins overheard this last request, and grabbing the chance for more organising of the troops, cheerfully bellowed the instruction to all and sundry.

"Will we be able to go after speaking to them?" whispered Martin Bramwell. "Only Dorothy's in quite a state. Someone should get her home."

On relaying this question to the sergeant, Colonel Simkins came back with the answer, "Yes. Dorothy, m'dear, would you like to go first?"

Dorothy walked to the kitchen as if she was walking to the gallows. A hush fell on the room - everyone feeling so awkward. Charity busied her *ad hoc* tea ladies pouring out cups of tea and passing round the milk and sugar. Hilda encouraged everyone to keep eating the Christmas fare Peter Threlgood had provided for them. "Shame to waste it," she said, through a mouthful of flaky pastry.

When Dorothy emerged from the kitchen again a few minutes later she looked shattered.

"Can I go next?" asked Martin Bramwell, "Then I can give her a lift home."

Dorothy stood in the middle of the room, her back firmly turned away from the dining room, whose door was now closed awaiting the arrival of the forensics team. She was shivering and Charity sat her down and plonked a cup of tea in her hands.

"Oh no!" said Dorothy suddenly, attempting to get up. "What about Toffee?" and she started to whimper.

"Don't worry about Toffee," said Tamsin, easing her back into the chair. "I'll take him for tonight. You need to rest. I'll talk to you tomorrow and maybe you'd like to keep him company after that? He's had a loss too."

Dorothy sniffed and dabbed her nose with a paper serviette. Fortunately for them all, Martin was soon out of the kitchen and took Dorothy away. The mood lifted very slightly, and people took turns in getting out of their chairs and entering the lion's den, Steve even attempting a bit of gallows humour. "Whatcher think, love?" he said to Dottie, "Think they've rumbled us?"

"Don't!" squawked Dottie, elbowing her husband in the ribs, "they may believe you!"

"Don't worry, Duck. We was well out of it." He cleared his throat and mercifully shut up.

Mark sat with his tattooed friend Manic. "Whaddya think, Manic?" he asked.

"Dunno," replied Manic, none too helpfully. He fidgeted endlessly with one of his bracelets, a chain with sharks' teeth, and attracted glowering looks from both the Colonel and Steve the tobacconist. Dottie had got up when Manic sat down beside her and pointedly took a seat the other side of her husband.

After three people had been interviewed, the SOCO chaps turned up, donning their protective suits and erecting floodlights for their photography. So there was a bit of a delay before the interviews resumed. They were mostly quite short, and everyone could hear what the Colonel said as he seemed to have adopted his parade-ground voice for the whole evening. If he could be heard over the roar of battle, he could certainly be heard in this genteel house!

"I agree with him," said Melanie, unavoidably listening to him. "I didn't see anything either. It's clearly an accident, so I don't know why there's all this fuss."

"I'm sure they're just doing their duty," Charity attempted to smooth Melanie's ruffled feathers. The last thing they needed was a mutiny. "The calmer we stay, I'm sure the sooner we'll be home. Oh, that must be the Rector!" She'd heard a tentative tap on the front door, a quiet, reverent sort of tap.

So Charity greeted the Rector, who looked suitably shocked and serious - doubtless having had years of practice at dealing with death and its aftermath - and took him to the kitchen door. As soon as Kevin Prenderghast came out from speaking to the police, she ushered the priest in and closed the door. He came out again almost straight away, accompanied by the constable who took him to the dining room and went in with him.

In the ensuing silence, heads were bowed as some folk joined in with the Rector's prayers in spirit. Others continued to sigh and fidget, and wondered how they were ever going to escape this nightmare.

The room gradually thinned out as the police worked through all the carol singers then let them go home, one by one. Charity, with the aid of Hilda, took charge of the WI ladies who, without tea to serve had relapsed into nervous anxiety, rocking and keening quietly. One of the last to be spoken to was Tamsin, who left the dogs with Emerald while she went in.

"Now, there's a familiar face," grunted the sergeant with a crooked smile. "I think you need an armed guard, Miss Kernick, given how often you find yourself amongst violent deaths."

"Ah. So it was violent then?"

"Have to wait for the post mortem," he said quickly, realising he'd put his foot in it. "But it doesn't look right."

"I'm guessing you'll want to clear it up before Christmas, then."

"You know the form!"

The constable came back into the room, having seen the Rector to the front door after his ministrations, and looked puzzled at the banter.

"This is Miss Tamsin Kernick," the sergeant enlightened him. "Just don't mention her name near Chief Inspector Hawkins." He winked at Tamsin.

"Come now, Sergeant, he should be pleased I'm here!"

"That's as maybe. Let's get a statement off you, anyhow." And he opened his notebook and asked Tamsin to account for her whereabouts throughout the critical time.

Having established where she was, where she remembered everyone else was, and describing what happened as she saw it, the sergeant snapped his book shut.

"Very observant you are. Now, off the record, Miss Kernick ...?" He raised an enquiring wiry grey eyebrow.

"Off the record, I'd say there are certain people you can totally discount straight away. There's Charity Cleveland, Emerald - and me, of course! I can't see those little old ladies from the WI doing anything bad, nor Electra Dodds." She shifted in her seat and gazed over the sergeant's shoulder at the door she'd seen Electra come through not so long ago. "Nor for that matter, Hilda. You remember her? She was one of the artisans targeted in that contamination business up at the Farmers' Market?"

The sergeant nodded slowly.

"And Shirley Vaughan - that's the one with the giant white dog - has enough trouble keeping her son Mark on the strait and narrow. Now I know Mark Bendick has a record, but I don't believe it's ever involved violence of any kind. Just stupidity."

The police both went "Huh!" The constable folded his arms.

"The young families had nothing to do with this, I feel quite sure. And I don't know the others at all well - oh, except for Melanie, the vet nurse, who I see when I take flyers in to the vets. And Kevin Prenderghast, who I only know as the owner of the insurance company, where that guy worked .. you remember?"

"The doping thing?"

"Yes, that one. So I can't tell you anything there."

"What about that lady," he flipped back through his book, "ah, here we are - Dorothy? She seemed to take it pretty bad."

"I was surprised, I have to say. She's a gentle creature - I know her quite well from lodging in her house for a while a few years back." The sergeant raised his eyes heavenwards. "And I knew she had a friendship with Peter Threlgood. But I didn't realise it meant this much to her. Poor woman. She's no spring chicken - perhaps she thought this was her last chance."

"She's lost her intended." He shook his head sadly.

"But she's gained a dog! I fully intend to pass Toffee on to her tomorrow. I'll hang on to him for tonight. In fact, could I raid the cupboards here and find his food and bowls and whatnot?"

"Technically we have to find if there's a family member who should take the dog. But as she already knows him well, it seems to make sense to let her have him. At least for the time being." The sergeant stood up. "You can get what you need when I'm finished here. Only a couple more to go, I believe." He motioned Tamsin toward the door, where she turned and added, "The dog needs to see Peter before they take him away."

The old sergeant looked up at her, took a breath to object, then thought better of it. "I'll take you in there myself, just you and the dog. Got it?" He added quietly, "Got a dog at home myself ..." Then, raising his voice he addressed his sidekick, "How's SOCO doing?"

The constable stopped picking his fingernails and jumped to attention. "They're just waiting on transport for the body, Sarge."

"Right. We'll have to secure the property when we're finished. So it looks as though we'll all be off soon. Be good enough to send in the next person, please, Miss Kernick."

## CHAPTER SIX

The next morning Tamsin woke up to some muted but sad howling from the kitchen. It took her a moment to work out what it was, as she'd know her own dogs' voices instantly. She could hear Banjo puffing slightly in agitation on the floor by her bed and suddenly woke properly as last evening's events flooded into her mind.

"Oh Lord!" She reached out a hand to some velvety muzzles and heard the thumping tails. "Poor Toffee. Doesn't know which way is up. We'd better go down and see him." She drew the curtains and looked up at the grey and sodden Malvern Hills. "It must have been drizzling all night," she said to her dogs as she pulled on her dressing gown. "Looks really gloomy out there. But it is December, after all!"

And as she arrived downstairs and let them all out to the garden, Toffee looking a lot happier now he wasn't alone, she heard the familiar dot-dot-dot of Opal coming down the stairs, just ahead of Emerald, who always seemed to float down the stairs silently.

"What a business!" said Emerald, opening the door for Opal to go out, nearly getting swept off her feet by a flurry of toffee-coloured enthusiasm racing back in. "Oh, I'd forgotten all about you!"

"He thought we'd forgotten all about *him*, poor lamb. Did you not hear him?"

"No? I was listening to whale music in my earphones while I did my yoga practice."

"Ah, yes, he did sound a bit like a whale! I'm going to get him over to Dorothy's today. She'll need something to occupy herself. And I want to see if she's ok."

"Did you know she was that sweet on the Churchwarden?"

"I had no idea. I'll have to grill Charity as to why she failed to keep me abreast!"

"You're on the trail again, Tamsin!"

"I am. Can't help it. There were plenty of good people there last night who need to be cleared of suspicion."

"And a few who .. perhaps won't be cleared?"

"Hmm. Has to be somebody ... Though we've no idea yet how he died." She tightened the belt on her dressing gown and thrust her hands into its cavernous pockets, fishing out an old chocolate bar wrapper and peering at it with a puzzled expression. "There's quite a crew of people I don't know too well."

"That friend of Mark's looked well dodgy."

"You of all people don't usually judge by appearances, Emerald?"

"He just looked so nervous. Very keen to leave."

"Can't say I blame him. He only came along to keep Mark company. He didn't know anyone else there."

"And suddenly he was trapped for hours, you're right."

"Perhaps he needed to go and feed his piranha fish!"

"Or listen to some heavy metal music to wash away the insipid carols! You going to start with Dorothy?"

"Yes. Need to check she's alright anyway. Dorothy gave me my start - I owe her. Then there's Charity. There really isn't much Charity doesn't know about people. And I want to talk to Electra too."

"Really? What do you think she knows?"

"It's not so much what she knows, as what she was *doing*." And Tamsin related what she'd seen in the kitchen the night before - a furtive Electra hiding something in her pocket. "Weird, don't you think?"

"Weird alright. Most weird. In fact, very very weird." Emerald shook her head in puzzlement and went to the back door to let the miaowing Opal in again, and this time an orderly procession of cold and damp dogs entered, each giving Toffee another sniff. Tamsin gave them all a cursory rub with a towel, put some of Toffee's food into his bowl and tossed a couple of handfuls of kibble to her own dogs to forage off the floor while Toffee ate his at her feet. Opal had parked herself on the worktop near the kettle, mewing plaintively as if on her last bushy legs, till Emerald jumped to it and filled her bowl.

Feeling much better after having got washed and dressed, and comforted by the steaming mug of coffee before her, Tamsin asked her housemate, "Where's the yogurt? We finished it?" as she dished up some oats and fruit.

"Sorry. I had the last of it yesterday. But we can get some of Susannah's lovely goats' milk yogurt when we go up there - whenever that is."

"True. Looking forward to that! Lots of fresh bouncy kids .. What are you up to today?"

"Thought you'd never ask," Emerald grinned impishly. "I've got an afternoon session, then I thought I'd help you with your Christmas Party at Nether Trotley this evening."

"Oh my!" Tamsin slapped her hand over her mouth. "I'd almost forgotten in all the hoo-hah! Thanks for reminding me! You'll be able to come with me this morning then. Dorothy first, I think, so we can offload this dawg. Just got to give these three a quick romp on the Common first, then we can get going."

When they arrived at Dorothy's, Tamsin holding Toffee's lead, his large bed under her arm, and Emerald carrying a bag containing his food and bowls, they were greeted by a dishevelled woman who looked so much older than usual. She'd clearly barely slept, with dark rings under her eyes, drained face and blank expression. "Oh goodness," she said, "I was worried about Toffee - I'd forgotten you were taking him, Tamsin."

"You never have to worry about dogs when I'm around! Where's Eddie?"

"He's in the kitchen. Doesn't hear much these days, he's getting on so."

"I love old dogs. And Toffee's a gentle fellow. They must have met before?"

"Er yes, they've met. On walks, you know." A little colour returned to Dorothy's cheeks. "Do come in while I put the kettle on. Is there any news?"

"Thanks, Dorothy. Nothing yet." And they all processed through to Dorothy's kitchen.

"Where will I put these?" asked Emerald.

Dorothy looked nonplussed.

"This would be a good place for Toffee's bed," Tamsin put it on the floor a little distance from Eddie's. "And I remember where the dog food is kept!" She found the cupboard and stowed Toffee's things, hanging his lead on the doorknob. "Keep to his usual food for a few days, Dorothy, then we can gradually change it if you like to the same as Eddie has."

"Oh look at them!" exclaimed Emerald. "They're old friends."

A sad smile crept over Dorothy's face as she watched the two dogs sniffing each other gently, their tails waving softly.

"He'll do you good, Dorothy," said Tamsin quietly. "Now, how about this tea?" And she set about making it herself, while Emerald spun her web of calmness over the grieving woman.

Once they were all seated in the living room, Tamsin quickly lighted the fire in the woodburner, fortunately already laid, and added some logs. With tea and biscuits to hand, Dorothy said, "It's all such a shock. Peter was a bit older than me, and had retired quite a few years ago. But he was in fine form. We'd go on long walks over the Hills sometimes, though the golf course - being flatter - suited me rather better." She smiled wanly and refused the biscuit Tamsin offered her.

"You *will* have to eat, you know," Emerald said, "You have two people depending on you now." She nodded her head towards the two dogs, both stretched out in front of the fire which was beginning to blaze well.

Dorothy gazed into the flames. "It's not as if we had an understanding or anything. We just enjoyed spending time together. I thought ..." She fished in her pocket for her hankie.

"We understand, really, Dorothy. He was a very nice person. Which makes me wonder - why anyone would do this to him."

"Do what, dear?"

Tamsin and Emerald exchanged glances, and Emerald moved a bit closer to Dorothy on the sofa. "They don't think it was a natural death." Tamsin said at last, with a sigh.

"Ohh!" and fresh sobs erupted from the shattered woman. "Someone *killed* him? I can scarcely believe it."

"Afraid it looks that way. That's why they spent so long interviewing everyone last night, after you left. We were there for hours. But until the post mortem is done, we won't know anything."

"Will you tell me when you know, dear?"

"Of course. But I expect the police will want to talk to all of us again."

"Is there anything you can think of, Dorothy? Anyone who didn't like Peter? Any reason anyone might want him out of the way?"

Dorothy shook her head helplessly, her now-damp handkerchief screwed up in her clenched fist. "He was a lovely man. I can't imagine anyone disliking him."

"Have a think over the next few days, Dorothy. Whether there was ever anything he seemed worried about. Or any mention of unwelcome callers, a voice from his past ... anything at all."

Dorothy nodded.

"Give me a ring if you remember anything, however unlikely. If someone did go to all the trouble of killing your friend, they must have a strong reason."

They sat silently for a few moments, gazing into the flames of the blazing fire.

Emerald, who'd left the room, returned with a cheese and tomato sandwich. "I made this for you Dorothy. It'll do you for lunch."

"Oh thank you so much - you two girls are a blessing." And she managed a half-smile.

"You may want a lie-down later. You must look after yourself!" Emerald spoke soothingly.

"And maybe a short walk with both your charges. A bit of fresh air is always a good thing. Magical healing properties!" said the more practical of the pair.

And so they left the sad house, glad that at least Dorothy had two dogs to look after now so she wouldn't be brooding.

"Electra next?" said Emerald as she clambered into the *Top Dogs* van.

"I think so. She has a little explaining to do! And I don't want her tripping up at her next police interview and incriminating herself."

"You'd have to be mad to imagine Electra could hurt anyone!"

"*We* know that, but *they* don't. And you know how they can jump to conclusions when they're on the hunt. Remember what happened to Charity by the riverbank that time?" Tamsin took off the handbrake and let out the clutch as they eased up the steep hill towards The Three Furies' house.

At this time of year, the Eastern side of the Malverns is in shadow virtually all day, the sun being so low the other side of the Hills. So this house always looked gloomy and damp, accentuated by the rough brown Malvern Stone it was built from and the era it was built in. Tamsin always felt that Victorian houses were designed to repel visitors rather than invite them! The double-fronted house had a fortress feel about it. It would have dated from the burgeoning of Great Malvern as a spa town in the 1800s, when people flocked there for the Water Cure. Malvern's famous charming gas lanterns erected in that period still dotted the road at night with their pools of yellow light.

But the outdoor appearance of the house was so different to the warmth and cosiness inside once you went in! Tamsin and Emerald were greeted with enthusiasm when they arrived at the house, which doubled as the premises of Dodds & Co, bakers *extraordinaires*. It was a house of two entirely different halves - the very old-fashioned decor, predominantly brown, with much heavy cream lace and many ornaments, and the sleek modernity of the stainless steel commercial kitchen which shone with a cleanliness that would satisfy any departmental inspection.

"It's Tamsin!" squeaked little Damaris, hopping up and down like a child, as she opened the front door to them. "And Emerald too!" She called her sister Penelope, who came lumbering from the kitchen, removing her overalls and hairnet and drying her hands.

"Come in!" large Penelope boomed at them.

"Thank you both - where's Electra today?"

Damaris fluttered, "Oh, she's got a headache - unusual for her. Gone for a lie-down." She nodded vigorously, like a little bird pecking.

"This nasty business has thrown her," pronounced Penelope. "You'd think singing carols would be safe. But apparently not."

"Not at all!" echoed Damaris.

"Too right!" agreed Emerald.

"Well, we won't stay," said Tamsin. "We really came to have a word with her about it all. See if she's ok. It was a big shock!"

"But resting in bed with her family around her is probably the best thing right now," Emerald added.

"Let us know when she's feeling better!" Tamsin reached for the front door handle. "Gotta fly now! Dogs to train!" and she let herself out.

When they got back in the van, they waved to Damaris, still standing on the doorstep, her head cocked, waving back vigorously.

"That was a disappointment," said Emerald, as Tamsin pulled away to turn the van back down the hill.

"Hmm. I wonder. She would be upset, naturally. Wonder why she got such a bad headache?"

"I don't like to think. Her actions were very odd. But there's nothing we can do about that for now."

"But you know what? It gives me a moment to call Maggie!"

" .. and find out what was so fishy about the Churchwarden's death!"

As they went back into their house in Pippin Lane, greeted with joy by the larger three of the four residents and a smug disdain by the smallest, Tamsin tried her friend Maggie - who just happened to be the police pathologist - on the phone.

"Gone to voicemail. I'll buzz her a text." And tapping away at her phone, she thought about what else she had to do that day. And realising what a lot it was, she started cruising the cupboards and fridge to find some lunch.

"That sandwich you made Dorothy looked so inviting!" she smiled, with a heavy hint. "Oh, here's something from Maggie!"

And while Emerald, who loved preparing healthy food, cut a few slices of brown bread, Tamsin read the reply.

*PM scheduled for 3. Patience, Grasshopper!*

She laughed as she flipped her phone off and fetched two mugs. "Post mortem is at 3," she relayed to Emerald.

As she placed the mugs on the table, she pointed to a teddy bear on the floor. "Tidy up, Banjo!" and the happy Border Collie scooped up the bear and plonked it on top of the pile of other toys in his toy basket. It was not too securely tidied though, and fell off a couple of times before Banjo managed to stuff it in with his nose, watch for a moment that it was not moving, and come for his reward.

"That's clever!" Emerald brought over the sandwiches. "When did he learn that?"

"Have you not noticed that there are fewer trip hazards on the floor this past week? We've been practicing for the party tonight!"

"Oh, there are tricks as well?"

"Oh yes! I always get students to finish up their courses by teaching their dog a trick, so they'll all be able to do one, however simple. I expect there'll be lots of roll-overs and play-deads."

"That's fun! I enjoy watching your dogs and their tricks. What are the others going to do?"

"You'll have to wait and see!" and they tucked into their lunch.

## CHAPTER SEVEN

After a delicious and very adequate lunch Tamsin was off again. She only had a few more home visits to cram in before the break, and two were that Monday afternoon. Through the narrow back lanes towards Halfkey she hummed happily to herself. This was really the best life! She was doing what she loved, all day long, and had to answer to no-one. Apart, of course, from her own conscience, which guided her through all the pitfalls and bear-traps you had to negotiate when dealing with people. The dogs were the easy bit!

Her first visit was to an East European street-dog that had been captured and carted across the continent in a rattletrap van and who was, unsurprisingly, scared of cars - and most other things, it had to be said. She made some considerable progress, largely in changing the new owners' attitude to, and expectations for, their unfortunate dog, and booked them into class in the New Year. "A little patience now will pay off handsomely in the long run," she assured them. And by the time she left, the cowering dog had relaxed slightly and was able to look his unthreatening visitor in the eye without flinching. The beginnings of trust.

The other call was right round the other side of the Malverns, on a country road near Eastnor Castle. It was a bread-and-butter visit to an eleven-week-old puppy living in a smart barn conversion with his new family. Nothing wrong with the delightful little fella, who was just being a puppy. Again, it was a question of educating the new owners and tempering their expectations that their tiny pup would be tramping over the Hills with them in a few weeks, walking to heel, fetching the post, and altogether being the perfect pet that it would in reality take some time to achieve. What people expected of their new dogs never failed to baffle her! They don't expect their three-year-old child to do calculus, she said to herself, so why can't they extend that thought to their little puppy or young dog?

Tamsin always delighted in working with new puppies, so she arrived home tired and yet refreshed by the work she'd done, and set about preparing for her usual Monday Nether Trotley class, which today would be anything but usual.

For it was the day of the Christmas fancy dress party!

Because it got dark so early at this time of year - it was already dark by four - Tamsin had walked her dogs much earlier in the day. Only two more days and the evenings would start to stretch out a couple of minutes a week. "Thank Heavens for that," she told the dogs, smiling at their puzzled expressions, "there is light at the end of this long, dark, wintry, tunnel!" she declaimed, and gave a dramatic shiver accompanied by a loud "Brrr!" causing the dogs to dance round her in excitement.

After a quick game with them, she got all their outfits packed and ready in one bag, with another bag for the cocktail sausages and cakes and biscuits and plentiful dog treats, with yet a third large bag crammed with rosettes and prizes and paper and pen to take note of the winners. So by the time Emerald arrived home, her offer to make coffee was more than welcome.

"Got everything ready?" she asked, as she got out the mugs and cafetière.

"As ready as I'll ever be ... *Oh no!* I nearly forgot the obstacles for the obstacle course!" And she thundered up the stairs to the spare bedroom which doubled as her dog-gear store, and started rummaging around the props box to load another bag.

"Now I could murder that mug of coffee!" she said as she humped the heavy bag down the stairs, narrowly missing Opal who darted under it just in time, and placed it ready with the others. The cat, who enjoyed living dangerously, hopped up onto the wobbly pile and started washing her long cream fur.

"Hey, Emerald," Tamsin said as she slumped into an armchair with a big sigh. "Could you be the official photographer this evening?"

"Course!" smiled her house-mate. "You going to send some to Feargal to print in the *Malvern Mercury?*"

"Good thinking, Batman! Yes, he must be back from his holiday soon. And they may find room for an amusing photo or two. Be sure to get lots of the children - the students have all given their consent to photos already, so we won't need to get it again."

"What did Maggie have to say?" asked Emerald.

"Oh Lord - I've had too much to do today - I completely forgot!"

"It's not late. You'd better ring her mobile."

"Let's see," she started to scroll through the contacts on her phone, "Oh how stupid I am?"

"You know you're very far from stupid. Not many detectives are running a dog school at the busiest time of year."

Tamsin grinned back as she heard Maggie answer. "Well? How did he die?" she asked her friend, picturing her in her scrubs and surgical cap - though as it happened she had just arrived at the shopping centre to pick up some food for supper, and was in her car.

"Wondered when you'd be on to me! But it's an interesting case."

"Tell us more! Emerald's here with me," she explained hastily, as she flipped on the speaker.

"Our Churchwarden died of cardiac arrest triggered by vagal inhibition."

"He what?"

"Someone exerted pressure on a specific place in his neck for a few seconds. Normally that would only cause him to lose consciousness.

But in the case of Peter Threlgood, his heart wasn't the best, and it caused heart failure."

"So he *was* murdered!"

"Looks like it. And murdered by someone who knew what they were doing."

"They had to have medical knowledge?"

"Either that, or experience - training, perhaps - in hand-to-hand fighting."

"Wow! That opens up the field. We had, er, two medical people there last night, a couple of burly young men, an army man .. Would they have had to know he had a dicky heart?"

"Not really, though it would have helped. They would presumably have continued to apply pressure if he hadn't keeled over. That would have done the trick."

"That requires a certain type of person."

"One that I don't like!" piped up Emerald.

"Ok Tamsin, you know we never had this phone call. We're just arranging a dog walk, right?"

"Definitely! Why else would we ring each other? And we must fix that up after Christmas! Love to see Jez again." Tamsin gave a wry smile as she rang off then turned to Emerald. "This really does help! There can't be that many people - especially in that small group - who know this trick?"

"I wonder if any of them had experience in the army, or commandos or whatever they're called?"

"Colonel Simkins for one, obviously. And what about karate and that sort of thing?"

"You know who probably does that?"

Tamsin raised a quizzical eyebrow.

"That friend of Mark's. Manic. He looked very strong and wiry."

".. showing off his muscles and *machismo* in his sleeveless t-shirt when we were all muffled in coats and woolly hats .."

"You'll have to find out if he does!"

"It's a pretty safe bet that something has made you think that."

Tamsin leant back in her armchair. "Oh my! Is that the time?" She jumped up, tipping Moonbeam off her lap. "We'd better get going. Give us a hand with these bags, would you?" And Tamsin loaded the dogs, kissing each one on the nose saying, "Break a leg!" and with a sudden burst of energy got all the bags and the photographer loaded up in the van, and they headed off in the dark to Nether Trotley Village Hall.

## CHAPTER EIGHT

Charity, who was born and reared in the hamlet of Nether Trotley, had only to walk up the lane to get there, so she was at the Hall first, and already had the room bright and warm. Once everything was unloaded from the van, Tamsin started sorting through all her stuff and laying it out on the table. Muffin and Tamsin's three dogs were happily snuffling about exploring the place, and Emerald went to help hanging the decorations from Charity's big box.

"No, you will not climb up on that step-ladder, Charity," she said firmly, arms folded. "Just pass me the stuff."

"Oh but .." Charity began.

"We're a team!" replied Emerald, standing on the ladder, "and you're best being the team captain and directing proceedings. You can see from floor level just how it's all looking."

Charity knew when she was beaten, and appreciated Emerald's way of affording her her dignity the while.

It didn't take the three of them long to get the Hall ready, and the first people started arriving with their dogs. Tamsin parked her three dogs on the beds she'd brought for them, and was happy to greet old friends, some who'd finished their classes much earlier in the year.

"Hello, hello, hello!" she greeted each of them warmly, "You're very welcome!"

"I wouldn't miss this for anything!" said Susan, as ever dressed completely in grey with mouse-grey hair and pale face, holding back her excited Frankie - who'd already dislodged his reindeer antlers to a jaunty angle and was treading on his red woolly scarf pompoms. "Hope it was alright to bring Mr.Twinkletoes too?" she asked anxiously, indicating the little Chihuahua in his red jumper bedecked with white bobbles.

"Of course! Delighted to see him again." Tamsin slipped each dog a treat. Frankie remembered to sit, while Twinks paddled all four feet on the spot with impatience.

Shirley burst through the door with her big white Luke, dragging behind her a sled bedecked with tinsel, its contents concealed by a cloth. "Ooh, you've got something grand there," said Susan, pointing to the sled, "I expect you'll win!" she said meekly. Shirley pushed her shoulders back and looked very pleased.

The Hall gradually filled with the sound of the tinny Christmas Carols coming from the speaker, and the hum of excited students and their even more excited dogs. But the level was ratcheted up 300% with the arrival of Chas and Molly, their four children, and Buster the Jack Russell.

Baby Amanda stayed in her push-chair brandishing her giraffe, while the boys all bounced up to Tamsin, trying hard not to all shout at once.

"Buster's got a new trick!" said Cameron urgently.

"I learned it him," said Joe, pushing in front of him, but quickly elbowed out of the way by his two bigger brothers.

"No, you never!" said Alex with a tone of outrage. "I taught him!"

"Boys, boys, boys!" Tamsin attempted to soothe them. "I know how much practice goes into getting a trick right. So it doesn't matter who taught Buster first," she winked surreptitiously at Cameron, who she knew would have done the teaching, "it's the practice you've all been doing that makes perfect."

Molly smiled warmly at Tamsin as the boys quietened down. "I don't know how you do it, Tamsin," she said quietly. "It just doesn't work the same way at home!"

"Ah, they know they can utterly depend on you to love them whatever they do," she assured Molly. "They can safely test the limits with you. With me they're still on their best behaviour."

But Tamsin knew that the boys all idolised her - and she'd heard Molly telling her husband before now how much she'd learnt about parenting from Tamsin's approach to dog training - 'slow to chide and quick to bless'.

"Come boys," said Chas, joining them from putting all their costumes on a group of chairs in the corner. "Time to get ourselves sorted! Tricks first, Tamsin?"

"Yes, we'll start with those - then there'll be some games, and we'll finish with the fancy dress parade."

The three boys jumped up and down and squealed, echoed by a squeal from Amanda, and they ran to their camp, Alex bouncing and almost tripping over Buster.

"Such wonderful energy they have," Charity had appeared at Tamsin's shoulder. "To think I was like that once," she sighed.

"You are one of the most energetic people I know, Charity," Tamsin chided her gently. "Though those boys take some beating! Molly is a saint. I think we're all here now - let's get started."

She knew some of the dogs would be spooked if she clapped her hands or shouted, so she turned down the cd of Christmas carols and made a trilling noise to attract everyone's attention and interrupt the chatter. She welcomed them all, explained briefly how the evening would go, and grinned at the surge of oohs and clapping when she told them it was tricks first. There was a flurry of activity as everyone got themselves ready, some doing a last-minute practice. Some of the dogs were paying attention, and some totally distracted by all the people and dogs around them.

But there was a great selection of tricks on show. Luke did a splendid 'Bang, you're dead!' albeit in slow motion, and was so comfortable lying on his side on the floor he had to be encouraged to get up again.

"Here, drop some treats just out of his reach," Tamsin said to Shirley who was trying to haul the big dog up.

"I never thought of that!" said Shirley, as, sure enough, Luke got up and lumbered over to hoover up the treats sprinkled a couple of feet away, and they continued to the side of the Hall.

Frankie did some nice spins on the spot, but sadly got confused with his 'Roll over' and did a kind of three-dimensional roll and spin simultaneously, which caused ripples of mirth in the delighted audience.

Banjo put some scattered toys away in his toybox, which mightily impressed Molly, who spent half her life clearing up after her brood; the two sausage dogs - Bertie and Percy - trotted neatly alongside each other like a pair of hackney ponies with Yvonne trotting along behind them; Suki, a small white poodle, pirouetted very prettily; Muffin fetched a ball of wool from Charity's knitting basket and brought it to her - "Oh you *clever* Muffie!" Charity said warmly over the applause; Ziggy the stiff-legged Fox Terrier's spins were all done as a series of enthusiastic bounces, enjoyed by all; Moonbeam did a handstand with her nose to the floor and her back feet stretching up the wall to the amazement of many, especially the boys, who clamoured to learn how to teach Buster to do that; and Quiz picked up an egg and carried it gently in her mouth to Tamsin, who - to demonstrate it was not a hard-boiled egg - cracked it into a bowl for her to eat. This brought gasps from the onlookers.

"My Tilly would've polished that egg off without bringing it back!"

"So would Jasper!"

"Oh, my fella would have dropped it and made an awful mess ..."

But the tour de force of the evening was definitely Buster! The three children set themselves up back to back in the middle of the room while Buster ran small circles closely round them, directed by Cameron. Then as the boys walked out into the room, Buster continued his circles which became bigger and bigger, until he was doing a great circle round the whole hall. Emerald, who'd been dodging about to get the best angles for everyone's tricks resorted to video for this one.

"What a wonderful way to use up energy!" said Shirley.

"Energy is something we're never short of in our house!" laughed Chas.

Everyone was impressed, and there was no question of who should win first prize. But everyone got a rosette and a prize for their pains, whether a dog biscuit with a red ribbon round it, or a fish-skin chew.

The boys were ecstatic.

"We won! We won!" Joe and Alex danced about, while the slightly older Cameron who, as a ten-year-old, felt he should be more adult, just beamed. He proudly took his little silver-coloured trophy to show his parents and little Amanda, who reached out to touch the shiny cup with wonder, before stuffing her giraffe's head in her mouth, kicking her legs and saying "Mm-mm-mm".

It was in a state of high excitement that they all took part in the games. There was the Fastest Recall (Banjo was the fastest by far, but the prize went to both Bertie and Percy who had definitely gone fast for their size and were the most comical, causing gales of laughter. Yvonne was tickled pink.). The Waggiest Tail (won by Frankie, whose tail hadn't really stopped waving since he arrived, much to Susan's delight), was followed by the Fastest Down (definitely not won by Luke, who took his time getting his great bones down onto the floor, then decided to stay there again).

A version of musical chairs, where both the handler and the dog had to sit, nearly ended in tears when Joe - who had borrowed Moonbeam to handle in the game - shoved Alex - who was accompanying Mr.Twinkletoes - off the chair, and was removed, protesting loudly, by his father. Emerald paused in her photographer role, and let this one pass unrecorded.

The mood was lightened again as they began the obstacle race, which had few rules but was a lot of fun. The dogs had tunnels to run through, some crinkly plastic sheeting to go over or under, a wobble board to wobble on, a sturdy box to climb on or into, and poles to go round.

"Oh, look at Joe!" Susan was holding her sides laughing as Joe clambered through the tunnels along with Buster. Instead of borrowing a dog, Cameron decided to push his baby sister's push-chair round the course, heaving her out to crawl through the tunnels, scooping her up at the other end and plonking the heavy baby back in her chair to carry on the course - causing much amusement for all.

"Those boys will be the death of me," laughed one older lady with a small fluffy dog on her lap, to her friend, who was dabbing at her eyes with a tissue, swaying with laughter.

And so they arrived at the high point of the evening - the fancy dress parade. Everyone had ten minutes to get their dogs ready, and waited nervously in line, tweaking and adjusting their dogs' costumes, often making them considerably worse. Emerald was on call to help with these. "No, you can't use a safety pin!" she explained to one person trying to attach a cloth to their dog's collar. "Unless you've got nappy pins. Ordinary ones aren't safe." And she solved the problem with some deft knots.

"Space them out a bit, guys!" called Tamsin, as she heard some grumbling from Bertie and Percy who felt beleaguered. Everyone shuffled apart so that the dogs felt happier.

It turned out that Frankie had come as a snowman, with his red scarf round his neck, and, still treading on the trailing pompoms, he held a carrot in his mouth. Luke's tinselled sled, once uncovered, carried a large cardboard barrel marked *Brandy*, with a smaller barrel hanging from his collar. This was greeted with warm applause, and a couple of cries of 'You can rescue me any day, Luke!'

The little poodle was a ballerina in a pink tutu and she carried a wand with a star and silver ribbons on the end. She kept dropping her wand though, so eventually her owner used it as a baton to direct her pirouettes. Lots of 'Aww's' for this one.

"That's so clever!" said Susan as the poodle team left the floor.

"You have to be clever to keep up with a poodle!" laughed Suki's owner.

Bertie and Percy's imaginative owner Yvonne had rigged up a cloth to their harnesses so that it was spread between them as they walked, bearing a teddy bear wearing a crown. Once mollified by getting lots of attention from people and less from dogs, they trotted proudly, though the bear did keep tipping over onto its nose and had to be repeatedly restored to the upright position.

Moonbeam was the cutest Mrs. Mop ever as she pranced along holding her dish-mop. "Can we book her to clean our kitchen?" called out the dachshunds' owner. And Banjo looked very dashing as a pirate, clamping his teeth hard on to his 'dagger' so he could focus on holding it tight and not have to worry about all the people looking at him.

Quiz brought a lot of laughs wearing the fleece as a 'sheep-dog', Muffin wore a polka-dot t-shirt and pulled a toy goat alongside her, which unfortunately kept falling over and was dragged along on its side. "She's Heidi! Up in the Swiss Alps with her goats," explained Charity.

And Buster, carrying a riding whip in his mouth, was wearing a tiny brown felt saddle with a saddlecloth bearing the number 1. He was led by Cameron as a 'lad' wearing a tweed cap, and behind him walked Alex in dark clothing and a very large top hat as the owner, along with Joe, in a jockey's cap and colourful shirt with the number 1 on the back.

This stunning entry posed a problem for Tamsin, who wanted to spread the prizes out fairly. So, after a quick consultation with Emerald, who'd been busy kneeling down to get good angles for the shots of all the competitors, she announced that there were joint winners - Suki the mini poodle for her ballet display, and the three boys and Buster for their racehorse. They were given soft toys for the dogs, and a small chocolate bar for each of the boys, who already had one silver cup. Suki's owner was delighted with her trophy filled with sugared almonds.

All the others got a chew or a biscuit for the dogs - all seemingly happy with the distribution of prizes, much to Tamsin's relief - and had thoroughly enjoyed their evening, now rounded off with all the food. Some had brought plates of goodies too, so there was a great party atmosphere, with even some sparkling wine for the non-drivers. And as the evening wore on, the hall gradually emptied, leaving that slightly desolate feeling.

"After the feast, the reckoning! I'm going to be worn out before the man in red arrives," sighed Charity as she got stuck into the clearing up, and Muffin, Quiz, Banjo, and Moonbeam did their bit with the crumbs under the food table. Emerald, who appeared so languid but was in fact full of energy, whizzed round with the large broom - happily herded by Banjo - while Charity filled a black sack with rubbish and Tamsin packed her bags again.

"That was a lovely evening," said Emerald, tipping the sweepings into the rubbish sack.

"If only all of life were so simple and innocent," Tamsin sighed.

"It usually is!"

"You have a short memory, Em! You know what happened last night."

"You're not tempting fate are you dear?" frowned Charity, leading up Muffin. "Turning that accident into a something more?"

"No. No no! I wouldn't dream of it. I didn't have a chance to tell you before the party, Charity, but it seems that Peter Threlgood was very deliberately murdered."

Charity dropped the sack and gaped at Tamsin. "No!" was all she could say.

"I'm afraid very Yes."

"What a truly dreadful thing. A man who devoted himself to the church. Shocking!" She tutted as she shook her head in denial.

"You liked him?"

"I did, I did. Everyone liked him really ... well, not everyone, obviously," she sighed. "He only took on the Churchwarden role a few years ago, when he retired. Before that he was some sort of civil servant. The Rector let something slip one evening after choir practice, suggested he was in Intelligence of some sort. And I tell you who else liked him .."

"Dorothy."

"Oh, you knew."

"No I didn't - not until it was all too late. Fancy not telling me this prime bit of gossip, Charity!" Tamsin crossed her arms and feigned fury.

"Well, my dear. It's not gossip when it's true, is it." She kept a straight face for a moment, then burst out laughing. "But really, poor Dorothy must be shattered."

"She is. We took Toffee over to her earlier on today. She's a shadow."

"Then I'll go round to see her tomorrow morning first thing."

And so, after all the excitement and fun of the *Top Dogs* Christmas party, they were in subdued mood as the three of them, laden with bags, led their dogs out into the dark little Village Hall car park, where they paused for a moment in silence as they remembered what had happened in that same car park not so very long ago.

## CHAPTER NINE

Tamsin was still at Pippin Lane when Charity arrived the next morning. The dogs flooded out of the living room, greeted her warmly, then returned hurriedly to the other room.

"What are they up to?" asked Charity at this unusual behaviour.

"Oh they're watching a film - it's a nature documentary about cows and deer and the like. They love it! Moonbeam particularly likes the ducks jumping into the water."

"Extraordinary. What will you think of next? Well," said Charity, unbuttoning her thick winter coat and sitting down at the table, then seeing Emerald wafting in from the living room, said, "Oh hello dear. I've just been visiting Dorothy."

"How is she today?" asked Emerald.

"And how is Toffee doing?" asked Tamsin, showing where her priorities lay.

"I think Toffee is a bit subdued, poor thing, but he gets on well with Eddie. As for Dorothy - yes, 'a shadow' describes her well, as you said last night. I'm going back there later on to get her out for a walk while it's still light. Muffin will be fine with the other two."

"Good idea, to get her out." Emerald nodded. "A bit of cold air will do wonders, and looking after the dogs gives her something to do."

"Didn't she say the other day that she didn't have any B&B guests over Christmas?" Tamsin tilted her head as she tried to remember.

"She did. She was planning to spend Christmas Day over at Peter's." They were all silent for a moment. "But I believe she has people due in the B&B next week."

"Get her back in the saddle fast! And I still have some home visits to do to earn my Christmas break. So I'm off out soon. But let me know if I can help with Dorothy, Charity - perhaps a dog walk with my lot?"

"I'll ask her this afternoon. And tell me what else you're up to - don't deny it!" Charity held up her hand to interrupt Tamsin, who gave a sheepish smile and then admitted, "You're right, I've got a few people I'm going to talk to."

"Hmm? And who would they be?"

"Just about everyone who was there, broadly speaking." She stood up and added, "There are a few in particular where I want to find out their history. You said the Rector suggested Peter was once in Intelligence?"

"You mean he was a spy?" Emerald's eyes widened.

"Well dear, I don't *know*. Just a possibility. Maybe I got the wrong end of the stick."

"So somebody at the carol-singing was a spy too?" Emerald was aghast as she mentally ticked them all off in her mind, then giggled, "I'm imagining Hilda furtive in a black hat!"

"It's .. a possibility, as Charity said. Though not Hilda, I'm sure! But maybe someone was jealous? Someone thwarted in love?"

Emerald started to count on her fingers, "Hilda, the two WI ladies, Dottie ..."

"Martin Bramwell?" added Tamsin. "Peter never married."

"Well that could include anyone," sighed Emerald, dropping her hands into her lap.

"But it could also have involved a business deal - he wasn't short of money," put in Charity.

"Or someone he was blackmailing ... Really, until we know a bit more we can't make any sensible guesses. But I'll tell you this Charity - in strictest confidence!" Charity nodded. "Whoever killed him had either medical knowledge or armed forces or espionage knowledge."

"A commando?" ventured Emerald.

"Could be. That's why we have to check out their histories."

"But surely the police will be doing that?" protested Charity.

"Of course they will, but some of my friends have been hurt by this death, and some have been implicated in it. So - you know me! I want to find out."

"And finding out before Chief Inspector Hawkins does is what will please you most!" Charity rose to leave. "Do take care, my dear. If this was what they call 'a professional job', you could be in danger."

"I appreciate your concern, Charity. And I'll do my best to stay in one piece! Gotta go - I'll walk out with you." And she shouldered her training bag, gave each of the dogs a touch, and left the house.

Tamsin's home visit was to a family in Guarlford who had unwisely taken on two puppies from the same litter and who were now dealing with the consequences. As so often happened, they'd been guilted into taking two: "The last one will be so lonely," they'd been told. Tamsin explained to them gently and with great care that this was one of the tricks used by those ghastly puppy farmers to shift their bedraggled pups fast. Only she didn't say it like that! What she did do was revamp the pups' living arrangements totally, to ensure that each puppy was reared and trained as an individual. "Yes, it *is* a lot of work," she agreed when they protested, "but it's necessary for the outcome you've told me you want. If you let them run wild together all day long, they'll never pay any heed to you! You don't want to be like the person who told me 'I wish we'd listened to you a year ago. Now we just have two hooligans'."

As she got back into the van, the plentiful tea she'd been given sloshing about in her tummy, she wondered whether the family would dismiss her advice or actually give it a go. "We can only do so much," she said to herself as she put the van in gear and turned it towards Dodds & Co.

This time, Tamsin managed to catch all three of The Furies sisters at home. Damaris fluttered about re-arranging cushions, books, and knitting, to make a space for their guest to sit down.

Electra looked up shyly from beneath her short dark eyelashes and her face seemed to go through several shades of pink and white before she offered to go to the house kitchen to make some tea.

Oh dear, thought Tamsin, more tea. But it was important for them all to be at ease, and, of course, this was the Furies' house, so there was a good chance there'd be cake too!

As indeed there was, as it turned out. A sensational new recipe they were trying, involving orange, lemon and a light creamy icing. So it was a while before the inevitable question from Penelope, who narrowed her eyes and said, "You're investigating, of course?"

"Not much gets past you, Penelope!" laughed Tamsin, munching her way through the tangy, melt-in-the-mouth, lemon sponge, nibbling the curls of candied lemon and orange zest with a blissful expression.

"Well, Electra was the only one of us there last night. Do you want to question her?" said the nothing-if-not-blunt cook.

"There is something I wanted to ask, yes," replied Tamsin tentatively. "Will we go to another room, Electra?"

For a moment Electra looked confused, then realising honesty was the best policy, she shrugged her shoulders and said, "Here is fine, Tamsin. And I know what you want to ask me."

Tamsin smiled encouragingly as Penelope and Damaris turned towards their sister and waited.

"You see, Peter and I were .. er, friendly .. a few years ago. And I'd given him a book." She sighed, closed her eyes firmly for a moment, then carried on. "It was a slim volume of poetry. Love poems." She gulped and now she really blushed, right down her neck. "I'd written in the book ..." She cleared her throat. "It was all a long time ago, really! Years. But when I saw what had happened, I thought it may be an idea to remove the book. I knew he kept it in his study, off the kitchen. And that's what you saw me doing, Tamsin."

"Where's the book now, Electra?" asked Penelope. "I think you need to back up this extraordinary story with a bit of hard evidence."

"Oh, no, really .." Tamsin began, but Electra got up without a word and went up the stairs, returning a few moments later with a book which she handed to Tamsin.

"Open it."

Tamsin flipped it open and saw the sweet and somewhat naive dedication Electra had written. It was dated nine years earlier. "That's absolutely fine, Electra. I'm sure no-one else need know anything about this." And she handed the book back to a very relieved Fury.

There was a palpable feeling of relaxation in the room. Damaris hopped up and refilled teacups, and the conversation turned to lighter matters. Electra looked as if she'd shed a load from her shoulders.

And Tamsin felt a lot happier about her friend as she left a while later to return to Pippin Lane to try to focus on carrying on with her yearly planning.

## CHAPTER TEN

"We're clearing out the old year and preparing for the new one," Tamsin explained to her dogs as she stowed all the Christmas party stuff back in the spare bedroom and came downstairs, sending all three of them thundering down first, to plonk herself in an armchair with her laptop to carry on drawing up new sheets for the classes to come.

"That means," she said pensively, as she chewed her lip and worked out course dates in her calendar - with the enormous challenge of juggling dates to avoid high days and holidays and still fit in the optimum number of classes per course - "that we're going to throw out *all* the old dogs and get new ones."

Emerald put her head round the living room door. "I hope that doesn't apply to cats and house-mates too." And she came in and stroked the dogs' heads. "Don't worry, she doesn't mean it. She'd sell her soul before parting with you lot."

"That is true, I'm afraid. I'm stuck with you all," she smiled down at her troupe.

"We really need to avoid you when you're working out class schedules, you get like a bear with a sore head."

"So would you! It's so complicated, you wouldn't believe it. I've been at it for days. But I always manage to crack it in the end. In fact, I'm up to July already."

"Got to schedule some *Top Dogs* walks and next year's Christmas party!"

"Don't worry. It's all in here. This year worked out very well, so I'm modelling next year on it. Shouldn't be too difficult. If only Easter wouldn't keep moving about ..." she sighed and cursed quietly as she shifted a whole course a week backwards.

"I suppose that's one of the advantages of drop-in classes for my yoga students. They just keep going all year."

"True, but it's a bit different. I have a set program for each level of student, and they need to see results. So structuring the courses is essential, really. Get us a coffee, would you, old bean? I won't be much longer at this, then I'm *done* till the New Year!"

She got up and stretched and wandered into the kitchen as Emerald skivvied with the coffee things. "I'd been so looking forward to days of nothingness - sleeping in, reading in bed, long walks over the Hills .." She sighed.

"Can't you still do that?"

"Got all these people to beard in their dens! It's a curse, this curiosity of mine."

"But you love it!"

"Yes. You got me! Fascinating to see what makes people tick. And it's very fulfilling - catching the bad guys, trying to put things right for the good guys."

"So who are the bad guys?"

"Easier to say who the good guys are," Tamsin leaned back against the kitchen cupboards and folded her arms. "They're pretty easy to spot."

"Really, everyone who we already know is a good guy, and all those people we aren't familiar with are possible bad guys?"

"Y-e-e-s. There were a few there who I barely know. That doesn't *ipso facto* make them guilty!" she laughed, as Opal started to wind herself round her ankles. If there was activity in the kitchen, the crafty cat felt there was always a possibility of food happening. Ignoring Opal, she went on, "I want to see if I can get to talk to Colonel Simkins today. Fancy joining me? I have a suspicion he'd warm to a pretty young thing like you."

"I'm just a commodity to you, Tamsin." Emerald feigned indignation, but it quickly turned to a grin. "Yes, I'll do my best to charm him for you."

"And after him, we could try Steve and Dottie. They run a shop, so they'll be around."

"And so will Kevin Prenderghast, with his insurance business."

"I imagine Martin Bramwell has appointments. We could try and catch him as he clocks off?

"Don't forget I have class tonight at The Cake Stop! But I could come with you tomorrow evening."

"Ok, we'll do him tomorrow, along with any others we don't get to today. Thanks for that coffee," Tamsin reached out to accept the steaming mug. "I'm going to have another go at these dates. The longer it goes on, the worse it seems to get."

"I'll leave you to it, then," smiled Emerald, heading upstairs with her coffee, Opal plodding up behind her, her tail erect in indignation at not having charmed another meal out of her people.

Tamsin adjusted the gas fire, put a blanket over her knees, and got down to work, determined to get her dates mapped out for the year. And after another hour and a half there was a tired whoop of joy from the living room. It was enough to get three tails waving and twelve paws a-pattering, and she ran out to the garden with her patient dogs, for a quick game with the various toys lying about outside in the grass. She finished up with some recalls, calling their name and running away fast, flinging out her arm with a tug toy for them to grab and tug as they caught up with her. They all loved this game!

By the time she came back in, rosy-cheeked from the cold and panting from her exertions, Emerald was putting on her coat. "Ready?" she asked. "What's the Simkins plan?"

"I thought we could turn up looking for reassurance. I don't expect word has got out yet about how Threlgood died. So we can protest our ignorance while poking about in his history. I want to know if he was ever in the SAS or a commando or something like that."

"SAS?"

"Don't you ever watch the telly?" laughed Tamsin. "They're the - um Special something Service. Some division of the army. Do all sorts of daring raids and attacks."

"Special Something Service. That'll go down well with him!"

"I remember there's an SBS ... that's the Special Boat Service - must be the Marines. So SAS - how about Special Air Service?"

"Sounds good to me. But perhaps just the initials will do."

"Hope so. Well, we needn't pretend we know anything about it."

"Good! Cos we don't!"

And they set off to Colonel Simkins' home. It was another of those large Victorian houses on the top road on the way to Great Malvern. "Wonder if there's a Mrs. Simkins," said Emerald as they pulled onto the steep drive. "Look, the house is already in the shadow of the Hills. It must get hardly any sunlight." She looked at the tattered dead stalks of plants in the ragged, somewhat neglected flowerbeds lining the drive.

"Let's hope Mrs. Simkins isn't a gardener." Tamsin pulled on the hand brake and felt the van relax with a long creak as she took her foot off the brake. "Glad we don't live plastered up the side of a mountain!" and she stepped out gingerly, reaching for firm ground beneath her foot.

The Colonel opened the front door himself. He was wearing what used to be known as a smoking jacket - a rather threadbare embroidered number with lots of colours, possibly reflecting service overseas. The splendid jacket was let down somewhat by the old tartan carpet slippers he had on his feet.

He scowled at the two women with no sign of recognition on his face.

"We're sorry to disturb you, Colonel Simkins, but we were at the carol singing - that awful night - and honestly, we were so impressed by the way you took charge .." Tamsin started, then blushed at her brazen attempt at flattering the old curmudgeon. But to her surprise, it worked!

"Ah yes, dreadful, dreadful. That's where the old training comes in, you know, being able to take over in a crisis."

"We were like headless chickens!" simpered Emerald.

"Natural enough, m'dears. This sort of thing's not for the ladies. Won't you come in?"

He turned on his heel as smartly as his carpet slippers would allow, and Tamsin and Emerald exchanged glances and followed him in.

They had plenty to look at and admire in the large living room they were shown into. It was cluttered with artefacts of every kind - brass tables from India, wooden carvings from Africa, portrait paintings. It was like a museum.

"Wow, you have quite a collection!" said Tamsin, looking about the room.

"My father brought most of it back," said the Colonel, gesturing them to a pair of faded tapestry Victorian parlour chairs. "We're an army family, don't you know. Father spent many years in the Far East and saw service in Africa and India too, back in the day when the sun never set on the British Empire." He actually pronounced it 'Em-pah' as he pulled his shoulders back. "Oversaw the end of the Raj." He harrumphed disapprovingly.

"And you followed in his footsteps?" asked Emerald, gazing up at him.

"The world moves on. I served in many places - the Falklands War, Northern Ireland ..."

Tamsin pricked up her ears. Those were two places which her quick researches - while snatching a welcome break from scheduling - had shown had featured the SAS. "That sounds so exciting! Did you go on secret missions?"

The Colonel shot his cuffs and generally preened himself as he said, "Important work, yes. Covert missions of course. Can't tell you much." He gave a brief smile.

"Ooh, were you in that Embassy Siege in London?" Tamsin turned wide eyes to him. "That was so famous - I can remember my parents talking about it for ages after it happened. They made a film of it, didn't they?"

"So I believe. But if I had been, I wouldn't be able to tell you about it." He smiled again, like the cat who'd got the cream.

"But that would explain why you were so capable on Sunday night!" enthused Emerald. "Did you know Mr. Threlgood was ill?"

"I always thought him pretty robust for his age."

Tamsin jumped in, "So did you think that poor Mr. Threlgood had been killed by someone?"

"Now what put that idea into your head?" he asked tersely.

"Well, the police thought that, didn't they? That's why we were kept there for hours, wasn't it? They wouldn't have interviewed everyone like that for a natural death," protested Emerald.

"I was not privy to what the police were thinking. But there *was* something a little strange. I know the paramedics weren't happy."

"That's so awful," Emerald looked forlorn. "We only met Mr Threlgood that evening. He seemed such a nice man. Have you known him long?"

"Good fellow, I agree. I've known him a few years now, since he became Churchwarden. Seems very capable - Rector relies on him. Popular in the parish."

"And you were there in the dining room when it happened?" Emerald's eyes were wide.

"Goodness me, no! I was *near* the dining room. But I was just refilling my wine glass at the table near the door. Didn't see it happen, if that's what you mean."

The Colonel was beginning to get a little defensive, so Tamsin felt it time to relieve the pressure a little. "Has your family always lived in Great Malvern?" she ventured.

He relaxed visibly at this turn in the conversation. "Three generations of Simkins have enjoyed this house," he declared proudly.

"So you must have known him well. I mean, I'm sure you're involved in parish activities - like the carol-singing for a start."

"It's important to be a part of the town. Contribute to the community, don't you know. Threlgood used to be a surveyor for the council. Retired with a good record, I believe. Sits on local committees, you know the sort of thing. Always been public-spirited."

"So who on earth would want to kill him?" Tamsin asked earnestly.

"I have absolutely no idea. Always assuming he was killed, that is. Maybe some strange illness he had." The Colonel harrumphed again. He looked as if he was beginning to tire of these questions, so Tamsin switched tack.

"Do tell us: what was the most exciting thing you did in the army - that you're allowed to tell us about, of course!" she giggled. And this opened the floodgates. The Colonel relaxed, gazed into the middle distance, and told of battles he'd been in, prisoners he'd captured, dignitaries he'd met, medals he'd been awarded, borders he'd helped to re-shape.

Tamsin and Emerald lapped these stories up. "You must miss it all - and you must miss talking to others who were involved - know what you went through?"

"You'd be surprised how many people here have some military experience."

"Really? Do you mean on Wednesday, at the carols?"

"Yes indeed. Let me see ... Steve. He was a Sapper."

Emerald tilted her head.

"In the Royal Engineers. Building roads, that kind of thing."

Emerald smiled and nodded.

"Then there's Bramwell. He did a stint in the services. Wasn't for him. Preferred bending people's backs to going on manoeuvres. Oh, and Prenderghast ran the CCF at one of the local boarding schools for a while."

Before Emerald could look baffled again, Tamsin jumped in, "Oh I've seen them up on the Hills. Lying in wait behind bushes and things. Quite fun for the boys, I expect, being in a Cadet Force."

"Makes men of them," replied the Colonel, somewhat predictably.

"So there's lots of you!" beamed Emerald.

A big grandfather clock at the side of the room went through a sequence of purrings, squeaks, tings, and whirring, as it chimed the hour.

"Goodness!" Tamsin jumped up. "We've taken up so much of your time. We must get on! Dogs to train, you know," she laughed. "Thank you."

"Thank you," echoed Emerald, "That was fascinating."

"Any time, m'dear," said the Colonel expansively as he held the front door open for them. "Next time I see you, I'll tell you some more stories!"

They smiled and waved as they clambered into the van, and as Tamsin turned and pulled out of the drive and pointed the van down the hill towards town, she said through gritted teeth, "Not if I see you first ..."

## CHAPTER ELEVEN

"My goodness, what a strange character!" said Tamsin, exhaling noisily as she drove round Link Top, past Link Common, and down the Worcester Road to look for Steve and Dottie's shop. They found it not far past the Fire Station at the start of the Link run of shops - a very small frontage which seemed to have been squashed in between two larger buildings. A sign clearly sponsored by a chocolate manufacturer proclaimed *Newsagents and Confectioners*, compressed into the narrow space. The shop windows were covered with all the usual signs and stickers indicating that they were a tobacconist-cum-sweet shop, with a display rack of newspapers outside - and, curiously, a tub of children's colourful footballs - to entice shoppers in. Inside, the shop was crammed from floor to ceiling with shelving bearing basic groceries, unlikely things like mouse-traps and camping gas bottles, and a very large and very noisy tall freezer containing ice creams and some miserable-looking sausages and bags of frozen chips and peas.

Dottie was chewing the end of her pencil as she looked down at the cluttered counter behind a display of key rings and chewing gum.

"Hello Dottie!" Tamsin said chirpily.

"Yes dear, what can I get you?" asked Dottie, without looking up from her crossword puzzle book.

"Have you got this week's *Country Life*? I gather there's an article about training gundogs in it .."

"Nah, sorry. Don't stock *Country Life*. Don't 'ave much call for it," Dottie continued looking bored.

"Not to worry. Hey - weren't you at our carol singing last week?"

"Oh yes - thought I recognised you," lied Dottie unconvincingly.

"Wasn't it awful!"

"What a business, yeah! Quite upset me." She became animated at the prospect of some juicy gossip and leant forward over the counter. "They kept us there for hours and I missed my millionaire programme."

"Whatever do you think happened?"

Dottie looked nonplussed by this question. "Well, 'e dropped dead, didn't 'e."

Emerald had crept up beside Tamsin. "But they say he was *murdered!*"

"NO!" Now they had Dottie's full attention, and she pocketed her pencil and leant forward yet further, eyes sparkling. " 'Oo says that?"

"A few people have told me, so it must be true," said Tamsin, wincing at this dreadful logic. "Did you see what happened?"

"Nah. I was over the other side of the room with whatsername, the little old lady who organised it all ..."

"Charity?"

"Yeah. Charity, that's it. Me and Steve was talking to 'er. Can't remember what about. There was all that screaming, knocked it clean out of me 'ead!"

"So did you know him well, the Churchwarden?" asked Emerald.

"I didn't know 'im, nah. Not a church-goer, me. Our Steve had a run-in with 'im when 'e was working for the council. Something to do with putting up a lamp-post outside the shop. We said an' how we wouldn't be able to unload the stock if they put it there. Awful to-do there was, till they eventually decided to move it down a couple of yards."

"Goodness! Was he difficult?"

"Job's-worth, that's what 'e was," she said, using that favourite complaint about officialdom everywhere - 'That's more than my job's worth'. "So bound up in red tape 'e couldn't see what we was on about. Any'ow, Steve got him sorted. 'E's got no time for people like that. Safe job in the council, I asks yer. Doesn't know what it's like to work for a living." She set her face in an expression which conveyed that she and Steve had always worked especially hard.

"But Steve was happy to sing him a carol and eat his sausage rolls?" grinned Tamsin.

"Gotta get it where you can," shrugged Dottie. "Ain't that so, Steve?" she said as her husband came through the store-room door backwards, turning and peering over the top of the large box of cigarettes and display of lighters he was carrying. Spotting Emerald, he looked at his two customers and said, "Here, weren't you at the carols last week?"

"We were! I didn't realise you had this splendid shop. That's great display shelving you have there," said Tamsin, nodding to the robust meccano-like shelves down one wall. "Just the sort of thing I need for all my work-gear."

"Steve can do anything with 'is 'ands. Ever so clever, 'e is," Dottie beamed. "On account of 'im being a Sapper," she nodded vigorously.

Steve looked a bit sheepish, then accepted the compliment.

"What's a Sapper?" asked Emerald, who now knew perfectly well.

"We'd build the roads and bridges for the army following us. They couldn't do it without us and our Bailey bridges!"

"Gosh - you must have been at the forefront of all kinds of battles," she fawned.

" 'S'right. Working under fire, that was us."

"It must have been *awfully* dangerous!" She moved a little closer to the counter.

Steve was captivated by her, and started to relate tales of his extraordinary bravery and courage in the teeth of the enemy. Dottie had heard this all before, and with a noisy sigh, turned her book towards her so she could carry on with her puzzle.

"And did you ever actually kill anyone?" Emerald's eyes were as large as she could make them.

"Oh yeah!" Steve pulled himself up to his full 5 foot 9 inches and puffed out his admittedly small chest. "Sometimes they'd jump us, so we had to be able to fight back - silently, you know."

"So you killed people with your bare hands?" gasped Emerald.

Dottie tapped her pencil against her teeth, then tutted loudly from behind the counter.

"Er, well, ah - we were taught how to. I never had to, I'm happy to say. All's fair in love and war - but it's not nice all the same. Glad I don't have to live with that."

"Oh, yes, that would be awful!"

"Some guys went to pieces later on. Bad business." He shook his head mournfully.

"Bet you're glad you're here in the Link now, only killing pests!" Tamsin pointed to the mouse-traps and smiled at him.

Steve guffawed loudly as he started to unload the cigarettes from his box onto the shelf at the back of the shop, accompanying his laugh with a grating cough.

"I bet you get through a lot of cigarettes?" asked Emerald.

"Yeah, makes it hard for me to give up, handling them all day."

"An' you been out the back smoking again, 'aven't yer." Dottie scowled at him. "You know it ain't allowed 'ere in the shop. *Yer breaking the law!*" she said shrilly. Tamsin felt sure that it was Dottie's law that was being broken, and recognised that the little woman depended on her husband entirely and wanted him to stay around.

She'd been reading the crossword puzzle upside down and thought it time to halt this pending 'domestic'. "Six across: Legendary Grand National winner tangled up in a death," she read out loud. I think you'll find that's MURDER, Dottie."

"Lemme see. Of course! Red Rum. The racehorse. Gottit!" and she waved a cheery goodbye as they left the shop and she fished the pencil out of her pocket again to fill in the letters for 6 across.

As they returned to the van, walking past the troublesome lamp-post, Emerald said, "That's another one who could have done it."

"We're not eliminating many, at this rate. Let's see how we get on with our local insurance agent, Kevin Prenderghast." And they set off up the hill again, to one of the little roads leading off Church Street - Great Malvern's equivalent to a High Street.

Having slid the van into the last remaining street parking space, which miraculously opened up for them as they arrived, they trudged up the narrow stairs beside the second-hand bookshop to Prenderghast's Insurance Brokers.

"Don't touch the hand-rail," Tamsin warned over her shoulder to Emerald following up behind her. She shook her hand in disgust. "It's still sticky."

"Cleaning not Prenderghast's *forte*?" replied Emerald, keeping her hands well away from the offending rail.

"Business doesn't seem to have looked up since we last came. This matting on the stairs is, shall we say, overdue for a change."

"Perhaps they're insured against people tripping and falling down the stairs?" Emerald quipped.

The office was quiet and empty as they approached the reception desk, where Tamsin was relieved to see that the garrulous receptionist they'd dealt with last time - when they were investigating the death after Emerald's yoga class - and who had had eyes only for the dashing Feargal, had been replaced by a plump middle-aged lady who hastily stuffed her knitting out of sight under the desk as they came in.

"We'd like to talk to Kevin Prenderghast please."

"Got an appointment?" the receptionist said abruptly.

"Er no, but it's to do with what we were talking to him about this week. It's a private matter - not about insurance."

The woman picked up the phone, pressed some buttons and said, "Name?"

Tamsin sighed at her ill manners. "Tamsin Kernick."

"There's a Mrs Kendrick here to see you. Says it's private."

"Kernick, Ms," said Tamsin, unheard.

"I'll send her in." The woman put down the receiver and said, "You can go in, he says."

"Where?" asked Emerald, looking at the array of doors leading off the reception area.

"The glass door over there." She picked up her knitting again, terminating the conversation.

"Good morning," said Kevin Prenderghast effusively as they entered his office. "Hello ladies. Ah, Tania isn't it?"

"Tamsin. And this is Emerald. We were singing carols with you the other night."

"Of course, I remember you both perfectly. Do have a seat. First time you've visited us?" he asked, once they were all settled.

"Er, no - I was here a few months ago, when you had that young fellow working for you .."

Kevin Prenderghast looked shocked as he remembered the incident. "Oh! Bad business. Bad business." He cleared his throat. "And what can I do for you today?"

"It's about Peter Threlgood. His murder."

"Murder! First I've heard of it. I thought he just collapsed. I mean, there was no sign of anything untoward."

Emerald's eyes widened. "Oh no, it seems he was *murdered*."

"I don't suppose he had life insurance, did he?" Tamsin jumped in.

"Just house and car insurance with me. I've been checking them over. Though I shouldn't really tell you that," Prenderghast looked confused.

"Only that seems to happen in films, doesn't it?" said Emerald eagerly, "That people get murdered for the insurance."

Regaining his composure, and sniffing a little, he said, "But we're not in a film. We're in Great Malvern. Much more prosaic. Now, how can I help you?"

Tamsin decided to try to steer this strange conversation back on course. "You were in the dining room when it happened, weren't you?"

"Oh no, not at all. I mean, I was over talking to the mothers of all those noisy children when it was discovered - or, at least, *they* were talking to me. They nearly fainted at the screams. I looked over and saw Colonel Simkins and Dorothy and that vet nurse down by the dining room. Then the Colonel asked me to call the police and ambulance, so I went out to the hall where the phone was. The dining room was all barricaded by the time I came back in. I'm glad to say I didn't see the poor man."

"We wondered .." Tamsin shifted in her seat and sighed loudly. "We wondered who might have the knowledge to .. to do this to him. I mean, it would have to be someone who knew how to kill people silently."

"And quickly!" added Emerald.

Kevin Prenderghast looked startled. "Well, I don't know at all. I just don't know." He really seemed to have little imagination, Tamsin thought.

"Were any of the carol singers trained in that way?"

"Trained assassins!" Emerald was warming to her sparky role.

Kevin Prenderghast frowned at her with distaste and turned his shoulders deliberately to address Tamsin, "Colonel Simkins is obviously a military man. I believe the shopkeeper was in the engineers. Simkins introduced us last night. They don't insure their business or premises with me." He coughed. "That physio fella, he did a stint in the services. He was telling me about it when we fixed up his professional indemnity insurance. So there you are!"

"That Manic, the friend Mark Bendick brought with him. I haven't seen him before."

"Once seen, I'd say, never forgotten," he said huffily, then lifted and dropped his shoulders.

"You don't like his tattoos?" asked Emerald.

"Or his jewellery?"

"I do not! Goodness knows what point he's trying to prove, by looking so odd."

"You prefer a suit and tie?" Tamsin suppressed a giggle.

"I do."

"And what about you?" Emerald said quietly.

"We heard you have military experience," said Tamsin.

"Me? Oh!" he blustered. "You can hardly count that! I helped out with the CCF at one of the local boarding schools for a few years."

"What's the CCF?" Emerald asked, inevitably.

"Combined Cadet Force. It's teaching youngsters the value of service - we run about in uniforms pretending to fire guns, you know?"

"So that's what they were doing on the Common! Frightened the life out of me one day, when they all jumped out of some bushes brandishing guns!" said Emerald.

"Frightened the life out of Banjo too," laughed Tamsin, "when they did it to me."

"I'm sorry to hear that. They really should be a bit more aware of the public. They have to put up signs when they're using a public space. Did you not see them?"

Both women shook their heads. Tamsin certainly had seen the signs, but wasn't going to admit to that, for effect.

Kevin Prenderghast stood up and started to walk round his desk. "What makes you think it was a military man, anyway?" he said casually. "What do you know about it all?"

"Like you said - there was nothing to suggest that he hadn't just collapsed with a heart attack or something. But we've heard that there was more to it than that. So *naturally*," she emphasised the word, as she stood up too, "it points to someone who knows how to do that sort of thing. I'm sure I wouldn't have a clue!"

"All very alarming," Prenderghast tutted. "And what's your interest in it anyway?"

"You may remember, that unfortunate salesman of yours ..."

"Ah, now I can place you!" His thin eyebrows shot up towards his bald head. "You were mentioned in despatches, as it were. Pictures of you in the local rag."

"That's me. And there are some wild ideas going round, possibly implicating friends of mine. So I wanted to see what I could find out."

"Don't you trust the police?"

"Oh yes, the police are great! But sometimes, knowing the people involved - it can make it easier to track down the miscreant. Even without DNA testing and fingerprinting and database searching and all the rest."

"You came out with a surprising solution that time, I have to confess."

"Let's hope I can do it again!" Tamsin chirruped as she and Emerald went through the door being held open for them.

"Watch this space!" grinned Emerald, as she tossed her long fair hair over her shoulder and followed her friend out of the building.

## CHAPTER TWELVE

It was a pleasant day on Wednesday - if a little chilly - with a weak white winter sun dappling the ground through the threadbare trees. Tamsin had a busy morning and early afternoon with three home visits to complete. First was a frustrated bulldog who kept humping his cushion, followed by a dog rescued from a puppy farm who was afraid of his own shadow (but was soon warming to Tamsin), and a lovely dog who was simply full of beans! A training program to engage his quick brain started to work straight away.

So at half past three before it started getting dark, Tamsin and Emerald, with Quiz alongside them, were striding along the top road towards the bike shop where Mark worked, when they saw a cyclist heading towards them at speed, not wearing the usual lycra gear, but a sweatshirt clearly emblazoned *Flying Pedals*.

"Hey, Mark!" Tamsin jumped up and down, waving one hand in the air vigorously, the other hand occupied with holding Quiz's lead.

Mark saw them - couldn't miss them really - and slowed down to a halt beside them. He was always a bit nervous round Tamsin, considering his own chequered past with the law. But since the business with the mountain bikers - and the fact that his mother liked her - he knew her now to be firmly on his side. So he gave a broad smile but with a guarded expression in his eyes.

"Out for a walk to warm up?" he asked. "Hello Dog," he said as an afterthought. "Thought you had a little dog?"

Tamsin nodded, "I do. Moonbeam, who rescued us just before you did that time. This is Quiz. You certainly look warm! Not in the shop today?"

"This is a customer's bike. Intermittent fault that we couldn't locate - only happens at speed. So I had to take it out for a fast ride, didn't I."

"Found the problem?"

"Yep! It's the .." he bent over to point to a tiny screw amongst the cables.

"I would have no idea!" Tamsin interrupted him before he could start explaining. Emerald understood all about bike maintenance having completed a course on it when she had a bikey boyfriend, but had found it very useful to play the dumb blonde, so she was careful not to nod wisely at what he was showing them.

"What do you think about that carry-on last Sunday?" she said instead. "Who'd have thought carol-singing was so dangerous?"

Mark wiped his nose on his sleeve. "Well the old geezer just died, didn't he." Seeing their expressions, he added with a note of alarm, "Didn't 'e?"

"Seems not, Mark. They're looking for a perpetrator."

"It weren't me!" he protested loudly. "Didn't even know him till we got there. Mum dragged me along."

"And Manic came to keep you company."

"Yer. Wasn't going on me own."

"I think it was jolly good of you to come and support the evening," Emerald smiled encouragingly at him.

"And you sing well, Mark!" said Tamsin.

Mark blushed a deep and unbecoming red. Really, he's just a big child, thought Tamsin.

"So what did he die of, then, if it weren't natural?"

Emerald spoke in a stage whisper, "He was assassinated!"

"By somebody who knew how to kill secretly," added Tamsin.

"I'm too stupid to do anything clever like that!" Mark's shoulders relaxed and he looked relieved. "If I was going to do someone in I'd bash them over the head with a spanner." He gave a broad grin and chuckled.

"Nobody's suggesting it's you, Mark. Clearly not your thing. But tell me about your friend Manic. He looks .. er .. unusual."

"Manic's alright. He's a good guy. Not that I've always been the greatest judge of character," he fiddled with the bike handlebars and looked sheepishly at Tamsin, who knew quite a lot about his past and his errors of judgment. "Actually, I don't know him that well, but there's something about him. Met him on the motorbike maintenance course, you know, that I .. er .. that I was on." He shrugged to disguise his discomfort. "He works at the main garage on the Worcester Road."

"Wiry looking fellow. Is he very fit?"

"Yer, he does one of them Kung Fu things, Karate or summat."

Tamsin's eyebrows rose.

"But nah - it's not him. He's alright. Last time I was round his place he was feeding a baby hedgehog he'd rescued."

"Aw," cooed Emerald.

"I'd love to see that! Where does he live?" And Tamsin made a mental note of the place Mark named. Easy enough to remember - over the second-hand shop near Barnard's Green.

"Hey, Mark! You were taking pictures of the carol-singing, weren't you?" Emerald asked suddenly.

"I was. I gave them to Mum to send to Charity. Why?"

"Oh, I just wondered if you took any inside Peter's house, at the party?"

"Nah. Only outside. We were too busy enjoying the grub once we got in out of the rain!" He laughed heartily.

"Fair do's," smiled Tamsin. "Not to worry."

They bade goodbye to the young bike mechanic and watched him expertly race back towards *Flying Pedals*.

"Not him," said Tamsin as she bent to stroke patient Quiz's neck. "But good thought about the photos."

"Not at all him," agreed Emerald, "but I think there's a baby hedgehog that needs visiting, am I right?"

"You sure are!" laughed Tamsin. "Who'da thought it. Manic likes to give the impression that he's hard as nails."

"Perhaps he's cultivated that image for a reason?" Emerald adjusted her scarf up over her chin. "Brrr! Standing still has made me cold. Shall we give Martin Bramwell a try?"

And they headed across the top of Church Street till they found a modest doorway between two shops in a venerable Victorian terrace, a well-polished brass plaque announcing Martin Bramwell's medical qualifications.

"Wonder if he has a receptionist-dragon?" murmured Tamsin as the door opened automatically with a beep on her giving her name to the little grey slatted box beside it. Just like Prenderghast's Insurance Ltd, this door led straight on to a flight of stairs. But unlike Prenderghast's, these stairs were well-carpeted and nicely lit, with pictures on the walls of restful landscapes and lakes. And the hand-rail was polished.

When they reached the waiting room at the top of the stairs, filled with soothing piped spa music and glossy magazines, they found no receptionist, but a sign requesting them to wait. It wasn't long before the door opened and Martin's head appeared round it with a puzzled expression. "I've just finished my last appointment for the day," he said apologetically, "How may I help you?"

"Hi Martin," Tamsin said chirpily, as he stepped through the doorway. "We were at the carols on Sunday, remember?" They'd shared a whole evening of carol-singing, then a further hour at Threlgood's house, and yet he hadn't remembered them. Tamsin wasn't sure whether to be insulted, or impressed by his egotism.

"Oh yes, indeed, indeed. Sorry, I was trying to fit you into my mental list of patients!"

"No, we're not looking for your professional services. I'm glad to say we both keep ourselves very fit with our work. But .. could we have a word?"

"Of course." Martin closed the door behind him and waved to the waiting room seats as he took one. "Glad to hear you're in full working order," he grinned. "Er, we don't really allow dogs in here," he eyed Quiz suspiciously.

"Oh she won't be any trouble. Lie down, Quiz."

And as the dog lay down by Tamsin's feet, Martin realised he'd lost that round and said, "What did you want to have a word about?"

"It's about Wednesday, Peter's death. You see," Tamsin hurried on before he could respond, "they're saying it was deliberate. Not a natural death. I mean that's what we all thought at the time, wasn't it?"

"Absolutely! That's shocking." He looked genuinely amazed. "Did they tell you that on the night? I've been so busy finishing up with my clients before the Christmas break, I haven't been in touch with anyone."

"Ah yes, you left early to take Dorothy home, didn't you. Well, it's because of her really that we're here."

Martin tilted his head expectantly.

"She's ever so upset," added Emerald.

"You see, she had, shall we say, *expectations*. She'd hoped she and Peter would become a permanent item. And now they say he was actually murdered, she's in fear for her own life!" Tamsin crossed her fingers behind her back at this prevarication.

"Murdered? I can't believe it. He seemed an innocuous enough fellow." Martin shook his head slowly.

"Had you ever worked with him?"

"As a client?" said Emerald.

"Or .. at all?"

"I had not. Not a church-goer myself any more. I was a choirboy at one time, that's how I came to be in the carol group. Once Charity Cleveland discovered that, there was no escape for me!" he gave a short laugh. "And he has never been a patient of mine."

"Did you have to get planning permission to set up your practice here? I mean, you can't alter these old buildings, can you."

"I did have to, but it was very straightforward. I've made no structural alterations, just decorated internally. Why do you ask?"

"Peter Threlgood was a surveyor for the council - before he retired. I just wondered whether you'd come across him in that capacity."

"Oh, no. I only dealt with the pen-pushers - filling in forms and the like."

Emerald, who'd stayed standing, had been studying the framed certificates on the wall of the waiting room. "You've done lots of studying!" she said admiringly. "Have you always done this kind of work?"

"For a long time. But not always." He studied his fingernails. "Did a stint in the armed forces. Didn't like it!" He looked up and smiled at them. "But you can do lots of training courses while you're there, and I started off with physical fitness, which led on to sports science - hot topics in the army!" he laughed.

"So they gave you a jumpstart to your career?"

"They did! Don't know why I signed up in the first place, really. I was feeling a bit aimless, just broken up with a girlfriend, didn't want to move back in with the parents, you know the kind of thing. Turned out to be the making of me."

"I suppose along with learning how to keep people fit and alive, you learned plenty of ways to do the opposite?" Tamsin ventured.

"Actually, I never saw active service - I was in logistics. Safely behind a desk. Moving personnel and vehicles and equipment around, with the right clothing and gear for the terrain and weather - it's pretty complicated." He sat forward in his chair, suddenly becoming animated. "Did you know one of the problems in the Crimean War was the complete collapse of the supply system? It was so bound up with red tape that food and clothing sent out on ships never reached the soldiers at all. They were starving and freezing and suffering from scurvy." Martin became excited as he detailed the catastrophic events of the century before last.

"Why did they have scurvy?" asked a shocked Emerald, whose diet was very important to her.

"They got two potatoes and one onion a month. I know," he nodded, seeing the look on Emerald's face, "it sounds appalling to us!"

"Oh I remember! That's when Florence Nightingale went out there, to work in the ghastly hospital," Tamsin said, remembering something useful she'd learned at school.

"That's right! But the main problem was that what got sent out to these poor men never reached them. Like, left and right boots were sent on separate ships, and one of the ships sank. So no boots in the freezing mountains. And the navy, who'd known about scurvy for ages, sent barrels of lime juice. And the public sent vegetables. But no-one would take official responsibility for them, so they all rotted on the quay."

"How dreadful! I see you're an admirer of correct systems."

"Very much so. Fortunately for soldiery at large, things changed after this appalling nonsense became public back home. By the time I was there, it was a very efficient and well-oiled machine."

"That is fascinating. Really! But getting back for a moment to Peter Threlgood - who do you think would have wanted to kill him?" asked Tamsin.

"And who would be able to do it in such a secret way?" Emerald added.

Martin Bramwell got up and gazed out of the window onto the busy street below, now lit by street lamps and shops in the evening gloom. "I honestly have no idea." He turned to face them. "I didn't know the man till I had my knees, so to speak, under his table. Charity roped me in to sing. Knows I like singing. Can trill with the best of 'em!" he laughed, as he stepped towards the door to the stairs. "I was talking to that baker lady and her friends when the alarm was raised. That's quite a shock, to think that one of that group had murder in mind ..." He opened the door, shaking his head.

Tamsin and Emerald stood up and handed him one of her *Top Dogs* business cards. "If you think of anything - will you let us know? I mean, the police may be interviewing everyone again for all I know.

But I'd like to put Dorothy's mind at rest." She remembered just in time what she'd said at the start of their conversation.

"Of course. Thank you for coming round."

They trotted silently down the carpeted stairs, Quiz running down ahead of them, and as they reached the street Tamsin and Emerald exchanged glances. "We're learning more about military history in the last couple of days than in the last twenty years!"

Emerald agreed. "But it's not getting us any nearer."

Tamsin took out her phone as they crossed the top of Church Street, passing the statue of Edward Elgar. The world-famous composer had lived locally which is why his name appears in so many streets and businesses around Malvern. Quiz paused to sniff the base of the statue, presumably well anointed by the male dogs of the town, but being a fastidious bitch she didn't add her own scent. The pavements were busy with people hurrying home for the evening.

"Time to muster the troops," Tamsin smiled as she started tapping out a message.

"For a council of war?" grinned Emerald in reply.

"This investigation is taking a strange and unexpected turn. There!" she said as her phone pinged, "Feargal's back! We can meet tomorrow - let's get this thing going," and to keep warm they marched fast along the top road, Quiz trotting quietly between them, as they discussed what vegetables they'd be having for dinner to ensure they stayed scurvy-free.

## CHAPTER THIRTEEN

"Your face is funny," laughed Emerald as she studied Feargal's suntan in The Cake Stop the next day. "It's like you're wearing white goggles!"

"I was. Wearing goggles, I mean. Jolly bright, skiing with all that snow and sun around."

"You're a kind of reverse Panda!" Tamsin put the tray of drinks, cake and toasties down on their table. They'd commandeered the armchairs in the full-length window of The Cake Stop, so Moonbeam and Banjo could watch the world go by from their mats, which Tamsin had pulled out of her shoulder bag for them when they arrived. The thin sun coming through the window cast shadows of the words *Cappuccino* and *Latte* across their bodies. "Perfect!" said Tamsin, "My dogs are tattooed with my favourite beverage!"

And as Feargal regaled them with tales of his mastery of the slopes, and how he'd escaped without breaking any bones, they started in on the food.

"Mmm, this cherry cake is delicious," Tamsin licked some icing off her spoon and closed her eyes. "The cherries constitute one of my 'five a day'," she grinned. "How's your fruit salad, Emerald?"

Emerald smiled beatifically over her healthy and vitamin-C-laden choice, while Feargal licked his fingers, having quickly raced through his toasted sandwich. He tossed his floppy red hair back from his brow and offered the dogs some crumbs while he drew his massive slice of coffee cake towards him.

"So you've been finding more dead bodies while I've been away? Can't leave you alone for a moment!" he smiled.

"It's nice to know I have some gifts - even an unwelcome one!" Tamsin outlined the story so far, along with Maggie's revelations. Feargal drew out his trusty notebook and opened a new page.

"There does seem to be a military feel to all this. But I can't see the connection with Threlgood. He was never in the army, was he?"

"Not so far as we know. And it's not just military people who could have done this. Two of the carol singers have medical training, and Mark's friend Manic does some kind of martial art."

"But you're right, Feargal," said Emerald. "We need to look at the victim more closely - find out why anyone would want him dead."

"I can do some sniffing. They'll be putting some sort of obituary in the *Mercury*. I can offer to do it. That'll give me licence to talk to his contacts - and see which of them was carolling on Sunday." He made a note in his book.

"I can talk to Dorothy again. Oh, look - Charity's arrived." Tamsin waved to her friend coming through the big glass front door, her small brown fluffy dog pulling ahead of her.

Charity nodded to the barista Kylie, who knew exactly what the old lady would like, then made her royal progress between the tables. It was slow and stately as she had to greet practically everyone in the café.

"Drop her lead!" called Tamsin, and the straining Muffin, released, ran straight to join her and greet her special friend Moonbeam.

"I'm so sorry I'm late," said Charity, peeling off her gloves as Feargal drew up another chair and offered Charity his armchair. "Oh thank you, dear! I ran into that girl Melanie. You know, the vet nurse who was singing on Sunday? She was just heading down to the vet's for her shift."

"And what did she have to say for herself?" Tamsin smiled at Kylie and made space on the table for Charity's cup of tea, handing her her card at the same time - "It's on me".

"Thank you, my dear. Well actually, she was a bit short with me, as a matter of fact. Didn't really want to talk about it at all. Odd, because she was quite different before, during the carols. Very chatty." Charity shifted a little in her armchair to make room for Muffin to hop up beside her. She was slender enough for them both to fit beside each other.

"Hmm. Wonder why? Will you be talking to her, Tamsin?" asked Feargal.

"I will. I can drop into the vet's with some more flyers. I'll see what I can find."

"And while you're that end of town, you have a hedgehog to visit," said Emerald, who now had Moonbeam on her lap.

"A hedgehog, dear?" Charity turned to face her.

Tamsin leaned forward. "It seems that that tough guy Manic has a soft heart, and is nursing a baby hedgehog. Gives me the perfect excuse to visit!" she smiled impishly.

"He's a rum fellow," mused Charity. "All those tattoos and bare arms in the middle of winter. Makes me feel cold just to look at him!"

"Maybe he has something to prove? That would explain all the butch appearance?" Emerald suggested again.

"Clearly you've seen something in him that I've missed," Tamsin said to her. "But you're right. He actually seemed very courteous and polite. Didn't fit the image somehow."

"And he had a very pleasant baritone voice too," said Charity. "He sang most expressively in the quiet bits."

"Ok, so you're doing the vet nurse and the karate king." Feargal scribbled in his book. "I'm doing Threlgood's obituary, so I'll be poking around his history. What about you, Charity? What devious plan do you have?" He gave her a crooked smile.

"I'll start with Dorothy. I was over there yesterday, of course. The poor thing is in such a state. But giving her Toffee to look after was a masterstroke, Tamsin. She's fussing around over him and Eddie. Nothing is too much trouble for them."

"Think she knows anything?"

"I'll see what I can find. I've also got a few other people I'm going to look up. At the church, you know."

"The Rector?"

"He's definitely on the list. He's been the incumbent for about twenty-five years. So there's not much that's happened there that he doesn't know about."

"Any word from your mole at the police station, Feargal?" Tamsin asked quietly.

"Not getting a lot yet. They don't seem to have any leads."

"They're not alone!" Tamsin gave a wry smile. "A harmless, friendly bloke. An unlikely group of carol-singing suspects. An orphaned dog." She shook her head sadly.

"You sound like one of the *Malvern Mercury's* headlines!" Feargal laughed. "And you've resolved the orphan dog story very quickly."

She nodded with pleasure. "Are the *Mercury* doing anything with this? I haven't seen anything."

"They're torn between upsetting everyone at Christmas time and announcing a big murder scoop. I think they're waiting for something more from Chief Inspector Hawkins - your old friend!" he smirked.

"I hope Hawkins is doing better behind the scenes than we are." Tamsin sighed. "But let's see how we all do with our tasks today - who knows what we may turn up!"

She finished her coffee and put the mug down regretfully. "We're getting very close to the Big Day, and I've promised to drop round to Chas and Molly with some presents for the children on Christmas Eve."

"We've got to fit in a visit to the goat farm too," Emerald reminded her. "Is there any chance we can get this cleared up in time?"

"Oh I do hope so, my dear!" said Charity fervently. "It will be such a load off everyone's mind, so we can all enjoy our Christmas without any worries. I do so love Christmas," she gazed at the sparkly images Kylie had applied to the front windows of the café.

"Me too," agreed Emerald, "I just love it."

And Christmas was rushing towards them, fast.

## CHAPTER FOURTEEN

Emerald had a yoga session to go and teach, so Tamsin set off down through the town to reach the Vet Clinic, glad she was driving as a steady cold drizzle had started. She always had a bunch of flyers in the van, so she grabbed a handful and went in. It was an old-fashioned vets, in what had once been a large family home with servants' quarters, and to reach the desk she had to plough through the small waiting room - full of damp and bedraggled dogs, cats, and what sounded like a bird scratching about in a covered cage. A trail of wet footprints led in from the front door. Looking about, she was surprised to see Dorothy there, sitting on her own.

"Dorothy! You ok? Where are the dogs? Are they alright?"

"Oh yes, dear, they are. They're getting on really well, such a blessing."

Tamsin continued to look round for Eddie and Toffee.

"They're not ill, no no no! I want to do my best for Toffee, so I'm just having his details transferred to my name, and checking up on his worm doses and so on."

"That's a great plan. Has he got a microchip? You may need to transfer those details too."

"Oh, goodness! I hadn't thought of that. I'll have to ask them how to do it. Such a lot to do ..."

"And how are you bearing up, Dorothy?" Tamsin asked quietly. "Did you have any thoughts after we spoke?"

"Oh, I'll muddle through," she said sadly, then sat up straighter and turned to face Tamsin. "But yes dear, I did think of something. I was going to ring you this afternoon when I got back. You wanted to know if I could think of anything odd or unusual about Peter recently."

Tamsin's ears pricked up. "Yes?"

Dorothy leant forward and spoke quietly. "Well, you know Peter has - had," she sighed, shrugging her shoulders before she went on, "a big collection of books?"

"Yes, bookcases everywhere!"

"He picked some up from a second-hand bookshop a little while ago. A big box of them that had caught his eye. He'd been going through them, reading some."

Tamsin nodded eagerly.

"Most of them he put on his shelves, and some he took back to re-sell to the shop. But there was one he seemed very interested in. He kept it in his desk 'for safekeeping' he said. He looked something up in it a couple of times when I was there, and when I asked him about it he stuffed it back in the desk drawer and changed the subject. Rather odd. Not like him at all."

"That is odd," agreed Tamsin. "And is that book still in the desk?"

"So far as I know, yes."

"And was it an old book?"

"It wasn't, no. It looked like an ordinary cheap paperback. Bit faded and tatty. I didn't see it closely enough to learn the title."

"That could be of interest, Dorothy. Good thinking. Anything else, apart from the book?"

She shook her head silently, and then her name was called out by the receptionist, so she nodded a goodbye to Tamsin and went to sort out Toffee's details.

The second girl at the desk called out, "Bramble Brimblecombe?"

An old man got up from his seat with difficulty and shuffled over to the open door, with his small old terrier plodding along behind him. Tamsin smiled at the dog's name. Perhaps the owner wasn't aware of the way vets call dogs by their name and their owner's surname - in this case an ancient Gloucestershire name. Or perhaps he was so fond of his own name that he chose something as similar as possible for his pet. A few others in the waiting room were smiling too. Nice to have your day lightened in such a simple way, she thought. She waited till the girl was free and went up to the desk, offering her leaflets.

"A top-up for you," she said brightly. And as the flyers were added to the rack, she asked for Melanie.

It turned out that Melanie was in the pharmacy area checking supplies. "Might I have a word?" asked Tamsin, putting her head in the pharmacy window, and in reply she got a less than usually friendly greeting from the vet nurse: "Come through." She nodded at the door to the side of the reception desk. This was not Tamsin's own vet, so she was unfamiliar with the layout. "I've got a lot of supplies to work through. You'll have to be quick."

Tamsin was taken aback by this strange attitude. She hadn't been that forthcoming at the carols, she remembered. Perhaps she just has a bad attitude in general, she thought to herself. Or maybe she doesn't like family Christmases and is getting tense? Then as she entered the little room she said aloud, "Hi Melanie, I was just dropping in some leaflets and remembered I wanted to ask you something."

Melanie took some packs of medications from a box and started putting them onto shelves.

"It's about last Sunday. You see ... Dorothy - you remember her in the choir? - well, Dorothy's really worried that now her life is in danger." Tamsin crossed her fingers behind her back again. Lying was pretty alien to her. "So I wondered if you had any ideas about what happened ..."

"Why should her life be in danger? He died of a heart attack, didn't he?"

"Er, no. No, he didn't. It seems his life was cut short by .. someone. And Dorothy thinks she may be next."

Melanie suddenly stopped unpacking the box and stood up straight. She looked Tamsin in the eye. "Are you saying that old bloke was *murdered?*" There was a quiver in her voice.

"Afraid so. Isn't it shocking! I'm sure the police will be interviewing us all again. But I just want to put Dorothy's mind at rest, so I thought I'd ask you - since I'm here! - if you'd seen anything." She gave a broad smile in the hope of melting the vet nurse's stern manner.

Melanie stared into space for a moment, then got busy with her shelf-stacking again. "I was stuck with that insurance geezer when it all kicked off. Boring the pants off me, he was. But he'd parked himself in front of the sausage rolls and I was starving. I didn't notice a thing."

"You weren't talking to the chiropractor?"

"Martin? No."

Tamsin noted that she couldn't remember Kevin Prenderghast's name, but had no trouble remembering Martin Bramwell's. "Do you know him? Seems a nice man," she said, encouragingly.

Melanie looked a little flustered. "Oh, I've seen him around. I don't *know* him. Now, I'll have to get on. I have to collect more supplies from the back. And you shouldn't really be in the pharmacy at all!"

"Of course! But if you think of anything you saw, could you let me know?"

Melanie gave her a challenging look.

"So I can put Dorothy's mind at rest? My number's on my flyers." She gave an encouraging smile.

The vet nurse grunted noncommittally, and Tamsin left the vets, frowning. She could see Dorothy turning into one of the side-streets further up the hill, on her way back home to pay attention to Toffee, having lost the chance for ever to pay attention to his master.

'Methinks the lady doth protest too much', she misquoted *Hamlet* as she drove the short distance down towards Barnard's Green, and wondered if Melanie had a thing for Martin Bramwell - and perhaps he for her. It certainly wasn't obvious that evening. But there was something in her vehement denials that didn't ring true.

Along with the fact that her story and Kevin's story didn't match.

She frowned more as she pulled up in front of the second-hand shop, old chairs and tables cluttering the pavement in front of it, along with a metal trolley with a broken wheel, and a big cardboard box adorned with prices scrawled with a fat marker pen, filled with small household items and a couple of tattered, butter-smeared, cookery books. Seeing the door at the side of the shop, she gave it a thump and waited.

" 'e's not usually back for another 'alf hour," said a voice from the shop entrance. "But you'll 'ear 'im when 'e comes alright!" A small thin man wearing a khaki warehouse coat leant against the doorframe with his arms folded.

"He's noisy?"

" 'e's not noisy, but 'is bike is," the man chuckled.

"Ah, gotcher. Can I have a look around your shop while I wait? I won't miss him if I'm in there?"

"Yer won't miss 'im!" the man cackled and stood aside to let her go in.

More clutter was the last thing she wanted, but Tamsin always kept her eye out for something for the house. And today she wasn't disappointed. It was dark in the shop and she picked her way carefully through the obstacles. There were old chairs stacked upside down on top of each other, a cheap wardrobe, parts of a pushbike, a foxed mirror with a chipped frame, some battered baskets. Then eventually, on the top of a dented metal filing cabinet she saw a lovely and rather expensive grey fluffy cat-bed. She pulled it down, sniffed it - it was almost new - and marvelled at the low price tag. This would make a lovely Christmas present for Opal. Just as she was paying the cheerful shop-owner, her words were drowned out by the roar of a motor bike.

"Toldya!" he gave a wide grin, revealing a missing front tooth. "There's Manic now."

Tamsin just had time to toss the donut bed into her van and reached Manic's door as he did.

"Oh hi, it's Manic isn't it?"

The young man looked up at her, surprised. He was clad in black motorbike leathers, and as he pulled off his helmet she could see a gold earring glinting below his buzzcut. "Oh, you're Mark's friend!" he said with a broad smile.

"Tamsin. Yes! I ran into Mark today and he said you'd saved a hedgehog."

"Found him in the gutter on the Worcester Road the other night. No place for a gentle little hedgehog. He was all rolled up in a ball of course."

"Someone needs to tell them that their spikes may work against predators but they do not work against cars."

"Someone should. Before they get wiped out."

"Is it that bad?"

"There's a third of them gone since the turn of the century. Several million a year get run over."

"That's dreadful! I had no idea it was so many. One of my dogs is fixated with them when they get in the garden - but she doesn't hurt them," she added hurriedly. "I put on some gardening gloves and lift them over the fence. Dear little things!"

"I'm just going to feed this one - want to come up?"

"I'd love that!" Tamsin spoke genuinely. She was really warming to this kind young man.

Upstairs, Tamsin was introduced to Tiggywinkle, clearly a very young hedgehog, its spikes just beginning to harden, while Manic prepared some food. "I call them all Tiggywinkle," he grinned. "Saves time thinking of new names."

"What are you giving him?"

"Tinned cat food. And a little milk. They do well on that. I gave him a bit of beaten egg last night too. He cleaned that up fast!"

"So how long will you keep him?"

"Only another day or so. I've got the fleas and ticks off him. The fleas don't matter because they're hedgehog fleas, and can't survive on other animals."

"That's a relief." Tamsin didn't want to be carrying fleas home to her brood.

"He's from a late litter - but he should be hibernating very soon."

"Where will you release him?" Tamsin was fascinated.

"I'll take him down some fields well away from the roads. There's a good organic farmer over towards Hanley Castle. That'll be a good place. No insecticides, so no poisons."

"And lots of tasty insects!"

"Exactly. I've released hedgehogs there before." He smiled as the hedgehog noisily slurped up the last of the cat food and started on the milk. "He was scurrying about in his box here last night, digging about in the straw. He's nearly fit to go."

"May I ask you something?"

"Course! Ask away." Manic tidied up the hedgehog's dirty dishes.

"Um," Tamsin began a bit diffidently. Then she thought, 'in for a penny, in for a pound' and said, "You seem a very caring person. Gentle, even. And you sing nicely."

Manic turned to her and raised an eyebrow enquiringly, wondering where this was going.

"So .. what's with all the tattoos and butch appearance? It doesn't fit!"

He smiled and sat back in the chair he'd been perching on. "You've sussed me out! The truth is, I'm not very tall, and I was bullied mercilessly at school. It was awful. I'd be useless in a fight, and had no way to stop them picking on me. So I developed this *persona* - just to frighten people off, really."

"Aahh! That explains it," said Tamsin with a cheery smile of relief, reflecting on the fact that Emerald had hit the nail on the head. She'd taken to this funny-looking person. Being kind to animals was a sure way to Tamsin's heart - despite Emerald's reminders about gruesome dictators who murdered millions but still loved their dogs. "Do you like dogs?" she asked suddenly.

"I do!" he beamed. "As soon as I'm in a position to get a dog I will. Can't here, though," he looked about him at his small room, lifted his arms and let them drop again.

"You must join me for a walk one day - I've got three dogs, and I have a sneaky suspicion you'd get on really well with my shy guy Banjo." She narrowed her eyes a little as she pictured the scene.

"I'd love that! I really would. Here, let me give you my number and we can fix a time."

So Tamsin left the little flat over the shop and started back home, with a fluffy cat-bed and a phone number. She'd lost a suspect, but felt that she'd gained a friend. And while Opal would be happy, this wasn't solving the murder in time for Christmas!

## CHAPTER FIFTEEN

"What news, Charity?" Tamsin, back home again, picked up her phone which showed Charity's frowning face in the photo on the screen. It was frowning because the old lady had been struggling to take a selfie at the time. Tamsin smiled inwardly - this image always amused her.

"I just thought you'd like to know, dear, that I've been visiting Dorothy again this afternoon."

"That's good. How's she doing?"

"She's doing pretty well, all things considered. She told me she ran into you at the vet's? She's keeping herself busy with Toffee - sorting all his paperwork you know. And she's bought a stack of new toys for him."

"Something good has come out of this tragedy, at least. Eddie's getting pretty old now .."

"Aren't we all!"

"No, Charity, you are not getting old. You have cracked the code and you're getting younger!" she laughed.

Charity simpered. "Now now, don't tease! There's something else I wanted to tell you too."

"Go on."

"It's the Christmas carol books. They need them at the church for practice tomorrow. So I'll have to go round to Peter's house tonight to collect them." In a low voice she added mysteriously, "I've acquired a key."

"I won't ask how. But I think you'd like a bit of help carrying the books to the car?"

"Oh, what a splendid idea! How kind of you to offer."

The two conspirators fixed a time to meet and Tamsin got ready to set off. "Moonbeam? Want to come for the ride?" She didn't have to ask twice as her little black and tan terrier danced with delight at the sight of her pink lead - unlike Opal, who had been sitting next to her food bowl, hoping that Tamsin's arrival home meant that food would be forthcoming.

And now the aristocratic cat turned her back on this happy scene and, poking an elegant fluffy hind leg straight up in the air, started washing her nether regions, pointedly.

Arriving at Peter's house in the dark, Charity let the three of them in - for Moonbeam came in too - and shut the door behind them to look around.

"Oh goodness, this place still has food everywhere. We ought to do something about it - it'll be stinking soon!" Tamsin turned to look at Charity, "but are we meant to be here?"

"That nice Sergeant said it would be fine as long as we didn't go into the dining room - look, it still has tape across the doorway, and I'm guessing they've locked the door. Let's get this mess dealt with first of all."

"Right you are. Oh, by the way, Charity - where were you when Dorothy let out her scream?"

"Am I a suspect, dear?" Charity's wrinkled cheeks dimpled mischievously.

Tamsin laughed, "As if! No, I'm just compiling a list of where everyone was, trying to see who was out of place, you know?"

"Let me think," Charity pressed her finger to her lips and turned round to visualise the room as it had been that night. "Yes, I know. I was over there near the mantelpiece," she stretched out her arm and pointed, "talking to that shopkeeper couple, Steve, isn't it? And Dottie. Odd pair."

"Right. That's what they say too. You've given them the perfect alibi, it seems."

"Wait." Charity frowned and put her finger to her temple, then wagged it. "I was listening to Dottie going on about the traffic in Malvern Link. I was watching her mouth closely because I found her cockney accent a bit hard to understand in all the chatter in the room. And when Dorothy yelled, Steve was there. But I couldn't say that he'd been there just before."

"Interesting. I'll make a note of that. He's definitely on my short-list." And she shook out the black sack she'd found in the kitchen, and started tipping things in.

"What about that young man, Mark's friend?" Charity glanced across from her table-clearing.

"Manic? I talked to him yesterday. He rescues hedgehogs."

" 'nuff said," Charity nodded. "He has to be a good soul."

"He's like one of those types of dog that people assume are nasty, because of how they appear. And as I know well, so many are big softies underneath all the chain collars and prick ears."

Moonbeam benefitted from a few still-edible morsels as they discarded the remains of the food and stowed all the glasses and dishes in the dishwasher, eventually setting it to run. Tamsin took the rubbish to the outside bins, wheeling the bin to the front of the house for whenever the next collection might be, while Charity located the vacuum cleaner, and after half an hour the place was looking clean and tidy again.

"Time to take out the carol books?" asked Charity.

"Not yet - I have something I want to check. In Peter's study. It's through here, just off the kitchen."

Moonbeam had found a small panda toy under the kitchen table, pounced on it and started shaking it, terrier-style. "Come on Moonbeam, bring it with you!" Tamsin laughed as she went towards Peter's desk.

She opened the drawers by turn, rummaging carefully in each one. At last she found what she assumed was the book Dorothy had told her about. She sat down and studied the cover. "Look, this book was important to our Churchwarden for some reason. It seems to be a memoir, by some explorer."

"Not your Arctic explorer friend by any chance?" Charity raised an eyebrow, and dodged out of the way of Moonbeam who was flinging her new-found panda in the air before capturing it and ragging it.

"No, I think he's on the strait and narrow now," laughed Tamsin. He's writing about what he actually knows! But this was written .." she flipped some pages, "fourteen years ago."

"Are there any marks, or dog-eared pages?"

Tamsin leafed through the book, being careful not to tip out any possible bookmarks. "Nope. Nothing that I can see. You know what, Charity? I'm going to take this home and read it. There's got to be some reason he was secretive about this. Ow, Moonbeam! That was my foot!"

She bent down and looked at where her little dog was crouching under the desk, staring intently up at her new toy. "Oh, it's got caught at the back of the desk drawers. Here, I'll get it for you." She got off the chair and onto her hands and knees, feeling for the trapped toy. "Hey, what's this!" She pulled out her phone and switched on the torch, shining it up under the drawer.

"There's something attached to the bottom of the drawer! Here Moonbeam, take your panda away." She tossed the toy to the little dog and crawled further in, twisting her head round to see. "It's an envelope! It's taped to the bottom of the drawer. I'm having this!" she said, and peeled the tape back.

She crawled out backwards from under the desk and waved the envelope at Charity, and as she sat down at the desk again, Charity handed her a paper-knife. She slit the envelope open carefully, and drew out the single sheet of paper within. They both held their breath as they read it.

"P.146," Tamsin read out loud. *"I'm sure I know who this is. Will ask him to explain himself, December 13."*

"Wow! Page 146!" Tamsin turned the pages quickly, and skimmed through the paragraphs. After a minute she leant back in the chair, "It doesn't make too much sense. I'm going to have to read the rest of the book first."

"This could be pointing to the murderer!" said Charity, in awed tones.

"It could indeed. We need to get this safely out of here." Tamsin slid the sheet back in the envelope, put it inside the book and wedged both into her jacket pocket, buttoning down the flap. "Good girl, Moonbeam! It was an inspired move bringing you along!"

Charity was already stroking the little dog. "Can she keep the panda, do you think?"

"Of course! She's earned it, and Toffee is plentifully entertained in his new home. Let's shift these carol books and lock up."

## CHAPTER SIXTEEN

"So I was up half the night reading the book," Tamsin was talking to Feargal on the phone as Emerald tidied up the kitchen and fed the ever-demanding Opal, who instantly replaced her yowls with roaring purrs as she put her head into her bowl of food. "And I'm whacked now, I can tell you!" She gave a huge, noisy, yawn. "I had to read all of it in order to make sense of the passage on page 146."

She was walking up and down the room as she spoke, then took a swig of coffee and carried on, flipping her phone to speaker so that Emerald could hear as well. "You see this geezer who wrote the book told the story of an event in the army where a soldier had dodged a court-martial by lying. Seems he'd lost heavily at cards the night before, then sent his victim - the fella he now owed money to - out on a sortie in an area that he knew was peppered with landmines. He claimed he didn't know."

"Nasty!" said Feargal, his voice tinny through the speakerphone. "The victim died?"

"Blown to bits. Thing is, there's little to identify the culprit."

"Can't we just ask the author?" asked Emerald, one hand on the cafetière, twiddling a strand of her long ashen hair thoughtfully.

"No go there, I'm afraid. I googled him this morning. Died six years ago."

"So what *does* he tell us?" asked Feargal, tinnily.

"You'll have to speak up, Feargal. The rain's hammering on the windows here. Er, it all happened in some unpronounceable place - I'll text you the name. Can you find out who was there? Which regiments, or battalions, or whatever they call them?" she shouted.

"Wow, I can hear that rain too. Definitely! I've got a mate who's an army correspondent for one of the big dailies. He'll know how to find out," said the thin scratchy voice.

"Brilliant. You've got the list of people involved in the military who were at the carols?"

"Yep," squeaked the voice on the phone.

"But even if we find out who was there, how do we know what the connection was with the Churchwarden," Emerald objected. "He was never in the military, was he?"

"Something attracted him to this book. Something made him read it, and something made him make the connection. Perhaps when Feargal's done his stuff we'll be able to make it too!"

"Ok, I'm going to get on to this right away," the distorted voice said. "It's a busy time of year, and everyone's trying to get away. It's Christmas Eve tomorrow! You do choose your moments ..." Even through the speakerphone, Tamsin could hear the grin in his voice and knew he was just teasing her. Feargal too loved the chase.

Tamsin ended the call and refilled her mug. Sitting at the table and drumming her fingers on it, she said, "How would he know who it was? How would our Malvern-based surveyor have an interest in what happened years ago in a foreign country? How did he recognise this weasel?"

"Perhaps it wasn't the weasel he recognised ..." Emerald said quietly, then looked at Tamsin with her large blue eyes. "Perhaps he knew the victim."

Tamsin jumped up, causing two dogs to jump up as well, and Quiz to lift her head off her bed. "You're a genius! I never thought of that!"

But as she sat down again, she said, "And how are we going to find that out?"

"Dorothy. She's our only hope. She'd been friendly with him for years. Maybe some pillow talk?"

Tamsin raised one eyebrow at the thought of Dorothy and pillow talk in the same sentence. "You're right. Let's get over there right away."

The thought was father of the deed, and they were soon pulling the *Top Dogs* van into Dorothy's drive. They could hear Toffee's robust barking as they knocked on the door. "Dorothy's acquired herself a watchdog! He must be settling in nicely. Now Eddie's so deaf it must have been pretty quiet round here recently."

"How lovely to see you, come in, come in!" Dorothy looked much better, the greyness beginning to leave her face.

"Did you manage to sort out Toffee's paperwork ok?" Tamsin and Emerald greeted her with a hug, and the dogs with friendly pats. Toffee, true to his breed, brought them one of his brand new teddy bears as he snuffled into it, his nose squashed up, his eyes squinting, his tail beating a tattoo on the kitchen cabinets.

They accepted the offer of coffee and biscuits, and Emerald helped get the tray ready as Dorothy busied herself with the coffee pot. Tamsin amused herself teaching Toffee to release his toy and catch it again. And into this happy domestic scene with appropriate chitchat, after a while Tamsin tentatively asked Dorothy if Peter had any military connections in his family.

"Oh yes!" she replied, and Tamsin's ears felt as if they pricked up like Moonbeam's big bat-ears. "He was not keen on the army. Quite resentful, really. There was a tragedy in his family - a few years ago now. His nephew, of whom he was apparently very fond, got blown up by a mine."

"How shocking!" said Emerald.

"What was his name?"

"I don't know actually. He didn't like to speak of it. Too painful. He mentioned it once in passing."

"Was it his brother's child, or his sister's?"

"His brother's. He didn't have a sister. They live somewhere near the New Forest now. I notified him, of course. He's waiting for the funeral date then he'll come up."

"So the boy must have been called Threlgood too." Tamsin murmured, realising how valuable this information was. A couple more questions showed that they had dredged the depths of Dorothy's knowledge of this family tragedy, and after some more chat they took their leave.

"Oh Tamsin, I meant to ask you ..." Dorothy hesitated before opening the front door. "Do you have any classes coming up that I could bring Toffee to? He's very good really, but I thought it would be nice - a chance to learn more about him. I know you make a big thing about the bond between dog and owner."

"That would be brilliant! Yes - there are new courses starting in the New Year. I'll send you an email. Good call, Dorothy!" Dorothy smiled, her eyes still showing her pain.

Tamsin was eager to get her new-found information to Feargal, and buzzed a text off to him as soon as they got home.

*Landmine victim may have been called Threlgood.*

"That should give him something concrete to find out."

"I'm itching to know who it could have been!" said Emerald. "I'm going to go upstairs and do my yoga practice, then I have presents to wrap for my Mum on Sunday."

"How are you getting to hers? Are the trains running?"

"No. No trains on Christmas Day. She's going to collect me around 11."

"Oh, that's a pity - I'll miss her then! I'll be leaving with this crowd at 10." She swept her hand over her three dogs. "There'll be a big gang at my mother's, and I promised to be there in time to help with the dinner. Expect I'll be on potato-peeling duty!"

"Let's hope we can get to the bottom of this mystery before then." Emerald sighed loudly.

"If we haven't, we'll just have to take a day off from sleuthing and let our hair down, like everyone else," Tamsin grinned as she pulled her coat on again. "Any news from Susannah about when to visit her goat farm?"

"Not yet. I don't want to badger her when she's so busy kidding. But don't worry, we'll get there!"

"And real life doesn't stop," said Tamsin. "But fortunately the rain has. I'm taking these dogs out while it's still light. Thank goodness we've just had the shortest day! The afternoons will start to stretch out a precious minute or so at a time."

Emerald paused halfway up the stairs. "And in no time it'll be midsummer and we'll have long evenings."

"And I'll be walking the dogs at ten at night, to avoid the heat of the day! Come on doggos!" and she pulled on her waterproof overtrousers and boots, rammed her woolly hat down over her ears, and headed out into the wintry drizzle, her head whirling with what they'd learnt so far.

## CHAPTER SEVENTEEN

By the time Tamsin got back home and dried herself and her very wet dogs, her phone buzzed. It was a text from Feargal.

*Got news. You at home?*

*Yep! Come round now,* she tapped back, and added another mug to the two waiting for the kettle to boil.

"Feargal's coming round!" she called up the stairs. Emerald's head, wrapped in a towel, appeared round the corner at the top of the staircase.

"Has he got something? Ooh, this is exciting! I'll be down in a mo," and she disappeared again.

Tamsin, her hand resting on the newel post which, for once, wasn't festooned with damp coats or garments waiting to go upstairs, carried on talking with a raised voice, "I've texted Charity too. I think she should be in on this. Hope she can make it." Then she heard the hairdryer start its whiney moan, and knowing Feargal's requirement for constant feeding, she set about making sandwiches.

"I really think he's more of a ruminant than a human being," she said, when Emerald came downstairs, Opal making her characteristic dot-dot-dot sound as she made her way down with her. Emerald was brushing her long barely-dry hair and plaiting it over one shoulder. As so often her very fair hair shimmered against her carefully-chosen clothing - today a turquoise velvet tunic, over dark green woolly tights.

"He's not alone," she grinned at her friend, admiring the growing stack of sambos on the dish.

"I've just been for a cold and wet tramp up hill and down dale! I need sustenance!" She put the bread knife away. "You know, I once heard a vet describe parrots as 'opportunist raiders' because of the way they would eat almost anything. Maybe that description suits him even better!"

The dogs started excited barking and Charity's small figure could be seen fuzzily through the frosted glass of the back door. Much to Moonbeam's delight and Opal's disdain, she'd brought Muffin with her, so there were four waving tails and one flicking tail as Charity took off her coat.

And when Feargal burst in and negotiated more excited greetings from the dogs, Tamsin hung his damp raincoat over the banisters and they all went to the living room which was warming up nicely with the gas fire on full.

In no time Feargal had wolfed several of the sandwiches and he was on his second mug of coffee before they got down to business.

"I've found the nephew. You're right - his name was Threlgood. Jeremy Threlgood. Sufficiently unusual name to find easily. Glad he wasn't called John Jones!"

"And?" said Tamsin, who'd been patient long enough.

"And, he was in the same company as .."

The three women gazed at him, mouths open.

"Martin Bramwell."

"Good heavens! And he said he was behind a desk for the whole of his service!"

"Someone's telling porky pies," Feargal helped himself to another sandwich. "He was definitely on active service when this happened. He seems to have conveniently forgotten a whole chunk of his army career."

"Did you learn more?"

"Not really. It never came to a court-martial. It was put down to poor communication - an accident. Our Mr. Bramwell must be a good actor."

"So it was as that book says - he sent Jeremy Threlgood out to a mine-infested area deliberately."

"How appalling!" Charity lifted her shoulders and dropped them, shaking her head slowly. "It sounds positively biblical."

"And all for a loss at cards," Emerald joined in with the slow head-shaking.

"Maybe he'd lost a lot of money - that he couldn't afford." Feargal reached out to Banjo and fondly put a hand on his grey and white shoulders.

"Maybe he'd *pinched* the money that he gambled away .." Emerald suggested, "then panicked as he couldn't pay it back."

"How would killing the unfortunate nephew get the money back?" asked Charity.

"I dunno," Emerald chewed her lip. "Perhaps he wrote an IOU to him which he couldn't fulfil."

"That's possible!" said Feargal admiringly. "That would be it."

"Who knows?" Tamsin put in. "The thing is, it seems that he caused this soldier's death, on purpose. The family all thought it was an accident."

"And then Peter Threlgood came across it in that book," Charity said quietly.

"I wonder if he spoke to Martin about it?" This from Emerald.

"That could explain it all. Do you think we've run our murderer to ground?"

Charity frowned. "I do know that Bramwell was talking to Hilda and her friends when the alarm was raised. They were near me while I was trying to understand what Dottie was saying. But I don't know where he was before that."

Tamsin nodded, digesting this information. "We need to speak to Hilda." She made a note in her notebook.

"And don't forget - we don't know where Steve was at the crucial time either," Emerald reminded them. "They may have known each other. Been on the same campaign or something?" She gave Opal a thoughtful stroke, eliciting loud purring. "But there would have to be a reason, after all these years, why Martin Bramwell would do such a thing," Emerald added, very reasonably for her. "I mean, how did Peter Threlgood know it was him? No name was mentioned in the book."

"You're right, Em. To need to kill our Churchwarden, he'd have to know that he knew. And how would he know as it's not in the book?"

"Maybe .." Feargal began. "Maybe Threlgood knew somehow that Bramwell was in the same regiment? He'd mentioned it one day, perhaps?"

"Or maybe .." said Emerald slowly, "maybe he was talking to Bramwell and mentioned that he'd found out who killed his nephew. When he hadn't, in fact."

"This is getting complicated!"

"Supposing he just talked about the book - or the event. He had no idea who it was, but Martin recognised that he was in danger of being rumbled." Feargal put in. Tamsin nodded approvingly.

"I imagine *he* must know about the book," said Charity, and Tamsin nodded. "Do you think he saw it at Peter's house and put two and two together?"

"I don't think he can have done. Peter did keep it concealed in his desk."

"Well," said Feargal. "We do know that Threlgood was very concerned about what he'd read in that book. It was always thought his nephew's death was an accident, him being in a place with all those mines. And there had also been a suggestion of suicide, or just plain stupidity. He was evidently keen to clear the lad's name."

"He must have been very fond of him," said Charity sadly.

"He had no children of his own. So that's why he made all that secrecy fuss about the book. I wonder what he planned to do next?"

"Maybe ... more maybe's I'm afraid," said Tamsin, running her hands through her unruly hair. "Maybe he knew Bramwell had been in Logistics and thought he may be able to find out?"

"Or - another maybe!" laughed Feargal, "maybe he just had an idea that Bramwell had been in the forces and mentioned it to him."

"And like you said, Feargal - Bramwell felt the game was up and it was only a matter of time before the cat was out of the bag!" said Emerald enthusiastically.

"Supposing he didn't speak to Martin Bramwell at all?" ventured Charity. "Supposing he was overheard speaking to someone else?" They all looked at her.

Tamsin said, "Now that's a possibility! But we'd need to know who, and where. I mean, can it have been just that evening, after the carols? It was a snap decision to murder him?"

"That might account for doing it in such a public place. Surely it would be easier to do it secretly when no-one else was around?" Emerald was being unaccustomedly reasonable.

"He may have felt that it was all going to come out that evening! That it was urgent to silence Peter."

"Whoever was in the dining room with Threlgood grabbed their moment." Feargal ate a crumb off his empty plate.

"But it was pretty foolhardy! Anyone may have come in at any minute!" Emerald's mouth was open again. Feargal glanced over towards her.

"Let's go back to Charity's overhearing idea," said Tamsin as she emptied the last of the coffee into their mugs. Charity followed her cue and poured more tea from her little teapot, a quaint handmade pot designed like a round submarine, with the name on the lid which doubled as the conning tower: T4U2. "Who may Peter have been talking to?"

"Colonel Simkins?"

"Kevin Prenderghast?"

"Dorothy?"

"Anyone!" said Tamsin crossly. "You know what? I think Hilda will be busy preparing for tomorrow's Christmas food market. She'll be at home. I'll give her a buzz now." And making kissy noises to her dogs, she went out to use the house phone in the kitchen, closing the door behind her and leaving the other three to carry on thinking.

They heard her winding up the call, and the dogs reacted to these recognisable noises by getting up and waiting for her to come back in to the living room. Quiz's tail was slowly swishing while Banjo's nose was pressed to the crack between the door and the frame. Moonbeam was happily lying next to Muffin on the dog-bed in front of the fire, snuggling her thin-coated body into Muffin's fluffy curls to get warmer.

Dog greetings, welcome-backs, you've-been-away-for-ages, had to be gone through as Tamsin rejoined them. "We've got to think again," she said as she waded through the welcome party and sat heavily in the armchair.

"Oh?" asked Feargal.

"Hilda is quite, quite, *absolutely* sure that she had been explaining all about the Saturday market to Martin Bramwell. He'd been asking questions about how you qualified for an invitation, how much it cost - lots of questions. That's why she remembers. She thought it a bit odd - more than usual polite interest, you know?"

"How does that fix the time he was with them?" asked Emerald.

"She'd gone through all this explanation - it took her a while. Then they heard the scream. She remembers that clearly."

"I'll be blowed," Feargal folded his arms. Then crossed his legs. Then unfolded his arms to push his auburn curls out of his eyes, then uncrossed his legs, shifted in his chair, and finally slumped back, looking temporarily defeated.

"Where do we go from here?"

"I'm going to get to bed," said Tamsin. "No, I don't mean right this minute! But after so little sleep last night I seriously need to catch up."

"I think it's a good idea to put it all out of our minds for a while," Charity put her cup down quietly on its saucer. "Let it all find its way around our brain - in and out of all those little cubbyholes and up and down those paths. You never know what might pop up!"

"Good idea," agreed Emerald, collecting up the plates and mugs and tidying them back onto the tray. "It *is* nearly Christmas - I want to have time to get excited about it!"

"What are you getting Opal for Christmas?" asked Feargal, a soft smile on his lips.

"Oh that's a surprise! I don't want her to hear," smirked Emerald. And covering her cats' ears she whispered, "She's getting a flirt pole with red and green ribbons on the end."

"She'll love that!" said Charity. "My Sapphire loves chasing hers. It has a little soft mouse on the end."

"And the dogs *love* theirs! I fixed an old teddy bear leg to the end of it."

Feargal looked bemused, having no idea what they were talking about. "Let's see what tomorrow brings. Who knows? Something may happen that makes it all crystal clear."

Never a truer word was spoken.

## CHAPTER EIGHTEEN

Tamsin got up earlier than usual the next morning, waking in the small hours with the awful realisation that it was Christmas Eve and she'd been so preoccupied with the *Top Dogs* party and the murder investigation that she'd totally forgotten to get presents for her nephew and nieces who she'd be seeing the next day. So she rushed into town wondering what would be left in the shops, cursing the fact that she'd left it so late.

The centre of Great Malvern was heaving. There were decorations adorning the streets, and skeins of pretty white lights woven through the trees. Carols and pop Christmas songs could be heard issuing from the open doors of the shops. Groups of teenage girls were hanging about outside the clothes shops, making sure to be seen in their glad rags. Their efforts were largely wasted though, as no self-respecting boy would be found dead amidst the Christmas shopping rush. Doubtless they were all hunched over their games consoles somewhere. And everywhere was the hustle and bustle of people with shopping bags and trolleys rushing from one shop to another. There were happy ones - those who enjoyed shopping and making it a social occasion, calling out jolly greetings to each other - and the not-so-happy ones, who hated shopping and saw it as an evil necessity. Tamsin definitely veered towards that group, unless she was buying leads and toys for her crew, of course!

She'd found presents for the children that she hoped they'd like. So hard when they lived up in Derby and she didn't see them that often. But she felt that a pretty top for the older girl, a book about nature for her younger, quieter sister, and a game involving racing cars for the boy should be acceptable. She couldn't resist getting him a practical joke book too, along with various smaller trinkets, sweets, keyrings, bracelets and so on for the girls. In her family they had the sensible agreement that presents need only be bought for children. But she liked to make a token gift for the adults too. And as the food market was in full swing, she picked up some pretty jars of jams and pickles with gingham covers for her mother and sister-in-law, and some bottles of local cider for the menfolk.

"Tamsin!" exclaimed Jonathan of *The Cider Flagon* as he served her. "Time for another lesson for Teal, wouldn't you say?"

She just had time to promise a post-Christmas email to her friend and to grab her purchases before his stall was overrun with more customers and she was jostled away in the crowd. It had been too long since she had last visited Jonathan and his Springer Spaniel, over near Maggie's place in Herefordshire. She waved her hand over her head in the hope that he'd see her being bundled away in the rush.

And as she passed *Hilda's Homebakes* she gave another cheery wave, but Hilda was absolutely swamped with customers and didn't see her.

Relieved to have managed all her shopping, she was heading as if drawn by a magnet towards The Cake Stop to put down her heavy bags and take a break. She passed the wide stone steps leading up to the Enigma Fountain and glanced up at the statue of the composer Edward Elgar, who had drawn so much inspiration from the Malvern Hills - those Hills that inspired her too - when there was a big commotion on the stairs. Some people were shouting as they grabbed hold of the railings. Others jumped aside. And a man fell headlong down the steps.

There were gasps and cries as he landed on a large pile of shopping bags at the feet of some plump ladies who'd clearly started celebrating Christmas very early. Recognising him and pointing at him as he blearily looked up at them, one shrieked, "Hope he was insured!" and they all cackled loudly, bending over and holding their sides. More sensible and sober people were helping the man to his feet.

Tamsin got closer and saw to her amazement that it was Kevin Prenderghast, the insurance man. He was clearly shaken and was rubbing his elbow and knee by turns.

"The steps are slippery after all that rain," a voice in the crowd said.

"People should watch where they're going," said another, less charitable, voice.

By the time she reached Kevin, he was thanking his rescuers, but looked greyer than ever.

"What happened, Kevin?" Tamsin asked as he tottered to a nearby bench and sat down dizzily. The crowd of helpers happily dissipated now someone else seemed to have taken over.

"I .. I don't know. I was just stepping off the top step when .. I don't know. But I'm sure I felt a hand between my shoulder-blades."

"You were pushed?" Tamsin craned her neck to look up at the milling crowd by Elgar's statue, but she knew it was hopeless. Anyone involved would have disappeared long since.

"Why would anyone want to push you, Kevin?" she asked earnestly.

"I've no idea." He passed a shaky hand over his brow.

"Look, you need to get home."

"No - I was just going back to the office. Clearing up some last-minute stuff you know. I'll go there."

"Is anyone else there? I don't think you should be alone. You've had a bad fall."

"Yes, Janet's there. My receptionist, you know."

"I'll walk there with you. She can sit you down with a cup of tea and make sure you're ok before you leave." And she scooped up her bulging shopping bags again and took his arm as he set off unsteadily to his office.

By the time she'd helped Kevin up his narrow stairs and handed him over to Janet, who showed a great deal of pleasure at having the task of looking after him, even going so far as to put down her knitting to cluck over him, Tamsin set off to walk home through the damp and gloom, her bags getting heavier with every step. But she'd hardly reached the Priory Gatehouse when she stopped, and quickly dialled a number on her phone.

"Hallo, may I speak to Steve please?"

"Sorry love, 'e's out. Can I 'elp? I'm 'is *trouble and strife*."

"Er no, it's ok. I'll ring after Christmas. Bye." She put the phone back in her pocket and frowned as she walked on, amused nonetheless by Dottie's easy use of Cockney rhyming slang in explaining she was Steve's wife.

She'd missed out on her coffee at the café so when she reached Pippin Lane she was damp, tired, and cross. She crashed through the door, through the sea of dogs, dumped her bags and yelled "Coffee!"

Emerald was soon ministering to her and listening to her story. "You've had a shock as well," she explained as she put on the fire and sat Tamsin down with a blanket and a small dog on her lap. "I'll bring in your coffee in a minute and you can tell me more."

Once she was equipped with a steaming mug of the necessary, and an audience, Tamsin revealed that she didn't have much to tell. "I saw him tumbling and I saw him sprawled on all those shopping bags at the bottom of the steps."

"Looks like those pickled ladies saved his life!"

"I think you're right. Good thing they'd been buying lots of clothes and blankets, and not saucepans or garden gnomes. Falling down a flight of slippery stone steps is no joke." Tamsin shuddered, and drew Moonbeam closer. "But there were so many people! It was impossible to know how it happened. I mean - he's pretty fit. Able, certainly."

"Running up and down those steep office stairs all day would keep him fit alright! Without touching the hand-rail," Emerald giggled.

"But he's quite sure he was pushed."

"Awful. And if that's true, there's got to be a connection. I mean it wouldn't have been someone who'd lost their no-claims bonus, or felt their premiums were too high."

"You're right. It has to be connected. But why on earth would anyone want to kill Kevin Prenderghast? I don't see where it fits in." Tamsin put a hand to her head. "You couldn't get me a headache pill could you, old bean?"

Emerald jumped up. "I'll get you a pill, then I'm going to leave you to have a doze. I think you should rest."

And Emerald had been right. Tamsin slept like a baby for an hour, waking, headache-free, to hear Emerald talking on the phone. "Em?" she called out, as she heard her end the call.

"Ah, you look better! Here, have a cat," and she plonked Opal on her lap next to Moonbeam. "That was Susannah. She says kidding is over at last and asked if we can go round tonight after supper. I said we could."

"Oh good - it'll be lovely to see all the newborn kids tottering about!" Tamsin stretched her legs out and reached her arms up over her head. "You're a clever little thing," she smiled, "I do feel a lot better. And I think some things have sorted themselves out in my mind."

"Yes?" said Emerald eagerly, sitting down on the sofa to listen. "Was Charity right?"

"About letting the information filter through all the cracks in our brains? I think maybe so! The only reason I can think of for anyone wanting to get rid of Kevin is because of something he knew."

"Or even something he didn't know?"

"You're right! It was probably something he didn't know he knew or didn't know he didn't know ... oh, this is getting all tangled up again!"

"Go back to before I interrupted you."

"Ok. Someone wanted him out of the way because of something he knew. So I was going over what people had been saying in my woozy mind, and .."

"And?"

"Can you bring me my notebook? I listed what everyone had said."

Emerald sprang up and was back in a trice with Tamsin's trusty notebook.

"Here we are," Tamsin flipped past the pages about dog tricks and ideas for classes as she shifted Moonbeam's bony elbows off her thigh. "Yes, that's it! Kevin said he was talking to Molly and the other mother, whatsername - Sandra. But look here - Melanie says *she* was talking to Kevin."

"That can't be right. Maybe she muddled up the time? What about Molly - what did she say?"

Tamsin ran her finger down the list. "D'you know? I haven't even asked her. She's clearly not a suspect, and I just haven't got round to it!"

"Didn't you say you had presents to deliver to the boys today?"

"Oh my! Where's my brain! Yes - I'm due over there sometime today. I'll ask her then. We need to know where Kevin was. What he may have seen."

"Or not seen ..." said Emerald, twirling her long hair with one hand while the other stroked Opal, who'd found her way across to her favourite lap.

## CHAPTER NINETEEN

With a sudden surge of energy, Tamsin jumped up, all the dogs jumping up too. "This won't butter me no parsnips!" she said to her baffled housemate. "Enough talk - let's get moving. You up for this?"

Emerald deposited Opal on a nearby cushion, stood up and saluted, "Yessir!"

"We've got a lot to do today."

"Right sir," Emerald stamped her feet.

"At ease!"

"Not sure what that means." Emerald grinned, but relaxed all the same. "We have to go and see Chas and Molly .."

"I want to check something with Kevin - and I think we should all put our heads together and crack this today!"

"Before we go to Susannah's," Emerald reminded her.

"That's like a different world! Yes, I'm really looking forward to that - the smell of the hay, and those sweet kids with their little querulous bleats! I'll run upstairs and throw some wrapping paper on the human kids' gifts. Down in a minute." And up she went, two steps at a time, with three dogs thundering up behind her.

"Your turn to come with us, Banjo!" she said to the excited Collie as she re-appeared ten minutes later, with a large bag full of presents. "Ready, Em?" and they all clambered into the *Top Dogs* van and set off for Lower Thatchall.

The level of excitement in Chas and Molly's house was phenomenal. They were greeted by excited barking and jumping from their Jack Russell, Buster. The boys all jumped about and shouted at once - they were beside themselves with anticipation of what the Man in Red would be stuffing into their pillowcases - already hung up in readiness round the fireplace. Little Joe took Tamsin by the hand and led her over to his pillowcase, stroking it fondly. "That's my-un," he declaimed and looked up at her with shining eyes.

The kitchen smelt delicious. "How do you manage to find time to bake, Molly?" asked Tamsin in genuine admiration.

"I've had three helpers today," she winked, as she nodded towards the dish of very strange-shaped tarts, with very uneven and slightly grey pastry. "Cameron doesn't like mincemeat, so instead of mince pies we have lemon tarts." Cameron beamed proudly.

"They look gorgeous!" said Emerald admiringly. "Which ones did you make, Alex?" she asked the nearest boy. And before an over-excited squabble could break out as to which pie was whose, Tamsin said, "And no mince pies means Buster can have one too!"

"That's one of the reasons, to be honest," agreed Chas, walking into the kitchen with an armful of fairy lights. "There's little hope of them not being dropped on the floor or left on a chair where Buster can reach them."

"We're not taking any chances with Buster getting ill, are we boys?" Molly laughed, leaving the room as a distant wail signalled that Amanda was waking from her nap. Three little boys vigorously shook their heads.

"Can I come?" asked Emerald. "I love the sight of freshly-slept babies!"

"Of course," beamed Molly. "She'll be a freshly-changed one too, in a moment."

Tamsin handed over the presents, and Chas put them all under the tree. Joe, being only five, couldn't resist picking up the present with his name on and rattling it. "Oh no you don't!" said Chas, taking it gently and reverently, putting it back under the tree. "You have to wait till tomorrow!"

Joe lifted his shoulders and folded his arms with a "humph", as Chas said *sotto voce* "though I expect 5 a.m. is about as far as we'll get before they wake up! At least while it's dark we can explain it's still night-time and snatch another ten minutes." He smiled softly to Tamsin with his pleasure and pride in his family.

"Hey boys," said Tamsin, "it's stopped raining - take Buster out for a game of footie! We'll watch through the window."

And with shrieks and whoops the three boys clattered out of the kitchen with their little dog, leaving an ocean of stillness and quiet behind them. Molly came back in, with Emerald carrying Amanda, who gazed at Tamsin with her big brown eyes before waggling her fingers and saying "Mm-mm-mm" to her mother, which apparently meant, "Food, please."

Molly took the baby and sat her in her high chair. Amanda kicked her legs and drummed her hands on the empty tray till Molly gave her a bowl of fruit chopped up with little chunks of cheese - which instantly gripped her attention - and said, "Well Tamsin, how's the Malvern Hills Detective doing? Cracked the case yet?"

Tamsin sighed. "Sadly not. But I'm determined to do it before the big day. And time is running out."

"What about your friend Chief Inspector Hawkins?" asked Chas, pouring them all a cup of tea.

"Haven't heard a word. It was Maggie who told me Peter Threlgood was murdered .. though I'm not sure how you knew?"

"We live in a village, remember?" Chas grinned as he raised an eyebrow.

"Of course. Silly me!"

"We've got some ideas," said Emerald. She ducked as there was a thud of a football on the window frame just behind her. Chas jumped up and wagged a finger at his sons, who chorussed "Sorry Dad!" and carried on playing.

"But we need to get something straight," Tamsin went on. "I know you were in the garden with the children and Toffee, Chas. I saw you come in just after the scream. But Molly - where were you?"

"Am I on your suspect list?" Molly asked with a grin as she gave her little daughter some fingers of bread and butter. Amanda was happily chatting and chanting to her food as she enjoyed it.

"That would be too easy!" giggled Tamsin. "But I'd just like to hear what you were doing."

"When Dorothy screamed?"

"A bit before if possible."

"Hmm," Molly frowned and mouthed silently as her finger pointed in different directions for a while. "Got it!" she said with triumph. "I was with Sandra - the girls' mother - and we were both with Kevin, the insurance guy. He was standing with his back to the window. I remember because I was worried he was going to trip on those long curtains. Sandra was asking him something about whether bicycles were included in home insurance, because that was what her daughters were getting for Christmas."

"Fancy talking shop like that at a social do!" said Chas.

"Bit *infra dig*, I agree. Anyway he launched into insurance-speak - how she had to check her policy, they all varied, it depended on where the bikes were kept, their value - gosh, he went on!"

"I bet you glazed over," laughed her husband. "I know your tolerance for that sort of thing is pretty low!"

"Too right. I was gazing round the room while he droned on. And I can picture it in my mind. I guess the scream fixed it for me."

"Fantastic! What did you see, Molly?" Tamsin sat forward eagerly in her chair.

"I could see Hilda and her WI friends. They were talking to Martin Bramwell. Heaven knows what they had to talk about."

"Hilda says he was grilling her about the Saturday Farmers' Market. At length. She thought it odd."

"Right. Agreed. Well, then, I saw you two on the hearth rug with the dogs."

"No surprise there," Chas smiled, giving his daughter's chubby face a wipe and handing her her water-beaker.

"Charity was over by the mantelpiece, just near you. She was listening to Dottie rabbiting on."

"And Steve?"

Molly screwed up her eyes. "Nope. Not seeing him."

There was the sound of an argument breaking out in the garden. Chas opened the door and leant out. "Tamsin and Emerald don't want to hear boys fighting!"

"Yeah!" Joe shouted back sternly. "Father Christmas might hear us!"

" 'kay Dad," said Cameron, the oldest boy, and they resumed thumping the ball about, the Jack Russell Terrier's white paws getting ever muddier.

"Where was Shirley?"

"Shirley ... Shirley ... Oh yes - she was carrying a big dish of food. She'd been offering it to her son and his strange friend, near the door to the hallway. She was just heading in our direction when .. when poor Dorothy screamed. She nearly dropped the plate!"

"So that just leaves Colonel Simkins," said Chas.

"And the vet nurse," said Emerald.

"I can tell you exactly where the Colonel was. He was right by the dining room door. That's where the wine was, and he was keeping close to that table for topping up his glass. I don't think he moved far from there all evening!" Molly grinned.

"And Melanie?"

"Yes. She was there too. Kind of behind the Colonel, near the kitchen door. Think she may have been getting a refill too."

Tamsin pondered this for a moment. "Thanks Molly - you're an incredible witness!"

"So observant," said Emerald admiringly.

"She don't miss much!" laughed Chas, winking fondly at his wife.

"She does not." Tamsin said firmly.

Molly frowned and added, a little diffidently, "I may be wrong, but I thought I picked up on something."

"Yes?"

"The vet nurse woman. She didn't talk to the chiropractor,"

"This sounds like the curious incident of the dog in the night-time!" Tamsin laughed, "About what didn't happen. You mean Martin Bramwell?"

"Yes, Martin. She didn't talk to him at all, but I'm sure I saw something. A look. A fizz. Something between them."

"Wonder why so secretive?" said Chas. "They're neither of them married, are they?"

"Not so far as I know," agreed Tamsin. "Odd. Thanks, Molly, I'll put that behind my ear."

"And run it by Charity?" suggested Emerald.

"Indeed - there's another woman with amazing powers of observation and intuition!"

And at the right moment they left the family to their Christmas excitements and set off from Lower Thatchall to Great Malvern.

"Here," said Tamsin, passing over her phone. "Can you text Feargal and Charity? We can meet them at Jean-Philippe's." And they drove through the approaching gloom with anticipation.

# CHAPTER TWENTY

Great Malvern was still heaving with people, its Christmas lights now sparkling as the evening drew in, and they had to park quite a long way off and walk in. "We could have left the van at home!" laughed Emerald. Banjo wasn't mad about the crowds, but he managed to keep safely between Tamsin and Emerald.

"First stop Kevin. See if he's still there," Tamsin said as she marched along the pavement, dodging the hurrying shoppers laden with bags.

He was still there, with Janet standing guard over her boss, like the boy who stood on the burning deck whence all but he had fled. "I'm going to run him home in a moment," she assured them. Kevin looked grey and too tired to argue.

"We just wanted to check that you were ok," Tamsin said cheerily. "That was a nasty fall."

He moved stiffly in his chair. "It was fortuitous that those merry ladies had bought so many soft things for me to land on!" he said, in a rare attempt at humour.

Tamsin and Emerald laughed obligingly. "And talking of ladies ..

you were with the two mothers just before Dorothy sounded the alarm that night, weren't you?"

"Yes, yes. I told you that, didn't I?"

"I think you did. I just wondered, from what someone else had said, the vet nurse was with you as well?"

"Now you're confusing me," he said, putting a hand to his head.

"I think you should leave him alone now," said Janet forcefully.

"It's alright Janet," Kevin sat up straighter. "This woman solves mysteries for fun. No, that nurse wasn't with us. I seem to remember .. ah, no, I've forgotten now." And he put his hand up to his head again.

"Are you sure you shouldn't go to A & E?" asked a concerned Emerald. "I mean, you may not have banged your head, but if someone pushed you hard in the back - perhaps you got whiplash! You may need treatment."

"A night's sleep is what I need," he said as he pulled himself up with an effort. "Time to go."

Tamsin and Emerald trotted down the dim, shabby, staircase while Janet clucked round her boss and locked up.

"We need that coffee!" Tamsin said as she and Emerald, Banjo tucked snugly between them, wove their way through the frenetic noisy crowds of shoppers towards The Cake Stop. And they were delighted to see as they went in, pulling off their woolly hats and unzipping their coats, that Charity and Feargal were already there. Kylie served them their coffees, and when they'd all managed to find enough chairs and squashed in round a table in the busy café, Jean-Philippe's deep voice sounded beside them, "*Mesdames, Monsieur,* tomorrow we are closed for *Noël*. This Raspberry Pavlova won't last till Boxing Day - the cream, you see. You would like?"

"Oh yes, we *would* like!" Feargal got up to accept the dish of Pavlova and the plates and forks on the tray Jean-Philippe held out for them.

"My very special customers deserve very special treatment," he winked, and with a gentle bow left them to their feast.

"Thank you Jean-Philippe! Merry Christmas to you too!" said Emerald.

Between mouthfuls and "mmmm's" Tamsin filled Charity and Feargal in with the details, with Emerald chipping in with anything she'd forgotten.

"So it seems that the prime suspect would be Bramwell," said Feargal, who'd been listening carefully. "I mean, if it was him who killed Peter's nephew, he'd presumably be interested in covering it up." He spoke quietly, though the busy café was sufficiently noisy that no-one else could hear him.

"And, interestingly, it's been suggested that Melanie, the vet nurse, may have something going on with Martin Bramwell."

"That's not a crime?"

"No, but it's strange if they're going to the trouble to conceal it - at least from us that night."

"Was it me who suggested it, I can't remember," said Charity, putting her fork down and dabbing her mouth with her paper serviette as she finished her helping of cake. "Only, I thought the very same thing."

Tamsin and Emerald exchanged glances. "You're a witch, Charity, so you are!"

"Nothing gets past Charity," Feargal turned and beamed at her. "So it looks as though Martin has more questions to answer." He frowned. "But where does this take us?"

"And can we get there soon?" wailed Emerald, who'd as yet barely touched her meringue. "I really would love to be able to forget this and enjoy Christmas Day!"

Feargal made as if to reach his hand out to her knee, then thought better of it.

"I think we ought to keep Steve in mind too," Tamsin said as she put a dot of cream on Banjo's nose for him to lick off, going cross-eyed as he did so. This never failed to amuse her.

"You think? Why?" asked Feargal.

"We don't know where he was before he joined Charity - isn't that right, Charity?"

"Well dear, I know he was there when Dorothy screamed," she winced at the memory, "but I can't say he was there beforehand. But he could have been ..."

"I'm sure you would have noticed, Charity," Emerald reassured her.

"*And*," Tamsin went on, "he wasn't at the shop at the time of Kevin's fall." In answer to the stares from the others, she added, "I rang the shop shortly after it happened. Not there. *'e was aht*," she mimicked Dottie.

Feargal leant forward with interest. "So why would Steve want to do this?"

"He'd had a run-in with Threlgood over the lamp-post outside his shop, remember? Maybe he has a short fuse, and it had nothing to do with the nephew or the book!" Tamsin suggested.

"That's always possible," Feargal agreed. "But Kevin?"

They all looked blankly at each other. "I just had a feeling," said Tamsin. "That's why I rang him. Know what? I'm going to ring him now." And so saying she pulled out her phone and dialled the shop.

"Hi Dottie, Tamsin here. I just wanted to ask you something. How did it come about that you were singing the carols that day?"

"It's that Simkins. 'E asked us, on account of Steve 'aving sung in the Engineers' Choir. Why d'you wanna know?"

"I was just wondering whether there was any other reason for Steve being there that night ..."

" 'Ere!" squawked Dottie, "You leave 'im alone. 'E ain't done nuffing. That's the thanks we get for turning out on a foul night .." Tamsin held the phone away from her ear as Dottie ranted.

"Oh no, Dottie, it's fine! That answers it exactly. And we were glad to have you! Charity hopes you can come next year." She backed out of the conversation and ended the call. "Phew! I poked a bear. I think the Christmas rush is catching up with her."

"And it doesn't get us any further forward. But," said Feargal, "back to Martin. There's two things. Melanie said she was talking to Kevin, while Kevin and Molly and Sandra are all quite definite that they were together before the body was found. No Melanie. Kevin says she was over by the drinks table."

"So does Molly," said Emerald.

"Then, *if* she's having a thing with Martin Bramwell, why all the subterfuge? What are they hiding? From us, or from everyone?"

"You seem to be suggesting that Melanie and Martin were working together," said Charity slowly. "That would fit in with Hilda's story, that Martin was showing an unusual prolonged interest in the Farmers' Market. Establishing an alibi, don't they call it?"

"They do. And he certainly did," agreed Tamsin.

"Can we go back to the war story for a moment?" said Feargal, his pencil poised over his notebook. "We know that Martin Bramwell was in the same group as Jeremy Threlgood. So, given everything that's happened, it suggests that he was involved in his murder. What did that piece of paper say, Tamsin?"

"The one I found under the desk? It said, um, 'I'll ask him to explain himself'."

"So Peter hadn't yet spoken to him. Interesting."

"He said he thought he knew who it was. Perhaps he got cold feet and hadn't asked him directly?" suggested Emerald. "Whoever 'him' was," she added quietly.

"We're back into 'Perhaps-land'." Tamsin sounded glum.

"No, no, we're going to crack this." Feargal brandished his pen. "It's all there in front of us. We just have to use our imagination!"

"You sound like a general marshalling his troops, Feargal!"

"General. Hmm. How about Colonel? If Threlgood didn't know how to find out the name of the evil-doer, perhaps he asked Simkins. He seems a good bloke. Reliable, by all accounts."

"Yes! And that's where Charity's idea comes in!" Emerald clapped her hands.

"That someone overheard him asking Colonel Simkins?" Charity asked.

"Yes, that's it!" Emerald was leaning forward eagerly in her chair. "Peter was determined to find out who'd killed his nephew. So he asked the Colonel if he could help him find the culprit. Maybe asked him to talk to a friend in the War Museum or army records or somewhere. And he was overheard, and someone wasted no time in shutting him up, permanently."

"Let's run with that for a moment," Feargal cast an admiring glance in Emerald's direction, then went back to his notebook. "Martin Bramwell, assuming he was the one who sent Jeremy to his death, was having a long conflab with Hilda and her baking friends. So it presumably wasn't him."

"But that's assuming that Peter asked the Colonel at the Carols!" said Charity.

"You're right. Could have been any time." Tamsin ran her finger over her plate to get the last morsels of cream, not forgetting to offer her finger to Banjo to enjoy, while they all relapsed into silence. "What's your mole got to say, Feargal?" she said eventually.

"Not a lot. I think they're all in the party mood and planning to interview everyone again after Christmas."

"I don't believe the police are that slack!" protested Charity. "I've always been impressed with their dedication to duty."

"I was being flippant, sorry. Yes, they're a good bunch at this station. They haven't got very far, anyway."

"I've just remembered something. You know Melanie rang me and asked if she could come to the Carols?" said Charity thoughtfully. "It was a bit last-minute."

"I didn't know that. She didn't make much noise, either, when she got there," Tamsin said. "She was meant to be singing the descants with me and a couple of the others, but I could barely hear her."

"You mean she had other reasons for joining in?" asked Feargal.

"Maybe she just wanted to be near Martin?" suggested Emerald. "Perhaps she's keen on him, but him not so much." She looked up from stroking Banjo's head, which was now resting on her leg. "But aren't we forgetting something? Why on earth would anyone want to kill Kevin Prenderghast?"

"You're right. Completely forgot that. How stupid! So what's he got to do with it?" Tamsin tutted.

"It's got to be something he knew," said Feargal.

"Something that Molly said made me remember 'the curious incident of the dog in the night-time', you know, the Sherlock Holmes story .. something that didn't happen."

"Oh yes!" said Charity, "the dog didn't bark."

"That's it. Something he didn't know he knew because it wasn't there."

"Something he saw!" Emerald piped up.

"Or something he didn't see ... I see what you mean, Tamsin, old thing."

"Bit less of the 'old thing' if you don't mind," Tamsin put on a mock-offended face, then grinned at Feargal.

"Steve wasn't in the shop just after Kevin's mishap," Emerald reminded them all.

"And Martin was not in the dining room at the crucial time. That's for definite."

"And Melanie is not being truthful about where she was," Charity added.

They all looked blankly at each other.

"Ohhhh," Tamsin looked exasperated. "We're not going to get any further this side of Christmas. I think we should all put it out of our minds and pick it up again next week."

"What are we all doing tomorrow?" asked Charity with a light voice. "Let's look forward to that. I'll be going to church in the morning for more carols! I took all the books back to the church yesterday. The Rector was delighted with what we collected for the tower fund - thought you'd like to know. Dorothy's coming round for lunch with her two dogs - I didn't want her to be alone ... I've no idea how Toffee will be with cats, but .. we'll manage! Then I'll be enjoying a lovely quiet time with just Muffin and my cats - oh and I'll be ringing my niece Sophie in Torquay later on - find out how her baby is doing."

"That sounds lovely, Charity!" and Emerald explained how she was visiting her eccentric mother's houseboat for a couple of days.

Feargal was visiting his parents, as was Tamsin visiting hers. And after exchanging a few stories of family dramas at previous Christmases - with the inevitable drunken uncle - they all left the café in a better frame of mind - not without massive farewells from Jean-Philippe and Kylie.

"We won't be gone long!" laughed Tamsin. "I for one will be back on Boxing Day."

## CHAPTER TWENTY-ONE

Tamsin, Emerald, and Banjo pushed through the crowds - albeit getting a little thinner now, though more frenetic - rounded the corner and bumped into the very person - Martin Bramwell!

"Evening, Martin," said Tamsin with a sunny smile.

"Ah, evening, ladies. Wait, that dog looks different." He looked accusingly at Banjo.

"That's because he *is* different," Emerald laughed.

"Er," Martin looked confused, then his face screwed up as he took a big breath and gave a massive sneeze into the tissue he'd grabbed from his pocket. "Sorry. Got a cold. Damn nuisance."

"That's a shame," coo-ed Emerald, "just in time for Christmas!" and as she commiserated with him, Banjo scooped up the scrap of paper that had fallen from Martin's pocket when he pulled out the tissue, and sat smartly in front of Tamsin with it in his mouth, proud of performing his tidying trick without even being asked.

"Whatcha got, Banjo Bunny?" Tamsin asked quietly, turning aside as she took the paper. It was a printed advice sheet from the vet. She turned it over and read, 'Think we're in the clear now - nobody knows a thing'. She frowned, then gasped. Then holding it printed side up, she casually handed it back to Martin. "Think this fell out of your pocket,"

"Oh thanks," he said absently, snatching it and stuffing it back into his coat. "Must have pulled it out with the hankie when I sneezed." His face crumpled again as another massive sneeze erupted. He waved his hand at them and passed on.

"He doesn't really look like a dangerous murderer," said Emerald looking after him.

"No. But someone else does. It suddenly all makes sense .."

"What makes sense?"

"Come on, we need to hurry!" Tamsin strode up the hill with Banjo, Emerald hurrying to catch up.

"Where are we going?"

"To the vet."

"You've got it, haven't you? I know that look!"

"I think I have." They reached the van and drove down the hill to the vet's as fast as the busy dark road and quantities of pedestrians allowed. It felt incongruous, pushing through these happy shoppers who were intent on preparing for the big day, on such a dreadful errand. And as they pulled up at the surgery, they were just in time to see Melanie emerging from the building, calling "Happy Christmas! See you next week," over her shoulder.

"I'm not so sure you *will* be seeing them next week," Tamsin stepped forward into her path.

Melanie's mouth dropped open, her expression was like a deer in the headlights.

"You killed him, didn't you. You used the medical knowledge you've learned in order to save lives - to end one."

Melanie's eyes darted frantically from Tamsin to Emerald, then she turned and ran.

"*TUG!*" shouted Tamsin, dropping Banjo's lead, and he raced after the vet nurse. Her arms were flapping wildly as she ran. The collie leapt forward and grabbed hold of her swinging bag. She fell with a crash into the hedge.

They caught up with her quickly. Tamsin rewarded Banjo for his efforts, handed the bag back to its owner, and picked up Banjo's lead, as Melanie sat up and began to weep.

Emerald squatted down beside her, an arm round her shoulder. "Why don't you tell us what happened? It must have been tormenting you."

"It's been so awful. And all for nothing," she wept. "He told me he didn't want to know. That two wrongs didn't make a right," she gulped out her words between sobs. *"I loved him!"* she wailed, and sobbed even louder.

They waited for a bit till she was calmer. "Start from the beginning," said Tamsin firmly, never very keen on dramatic waterworks.

"I fell for Martin. Really fell for him," she sniffed. "He's so good-looking," she turned red eyes to Tamsin, who glowered back at her. "I really wanted to impress him, but couldn't think how. Then at that party, Peter Threlgood was talking to Colonel Simkins. I was pouring a drink for Martin. I heard him, Peter I mean, asking the Colonel how to find out who was in his nephew's regiment. He said he was sure his nephew had been murdered and he wanted to find the culprit. And he told him the name of the regiment. I knew that was where Martin had served when he was in the army. I looked at Martin. His face was ashen, his eyes darting frantically about. His hand shook so much he nearly spilt his wine. Here was my chance!" Her eyes were strangely bright as she looked up at Tamsin, as if she expected an accolade for what she'd done.

She started to shred the damp tissue in her hands. "I hung around by the wine table for a bit, till Peter went into the dining room. I followed him in. He started on about his boring watercolours!" she spoke with scorn. "As he peered closely at one, I reached up as if to point at it, and .. I just pressed the nerve on his neck, held it for long enough." She looked up at Tamsin, seeking admiration for her deed. Tamsin remained stern and silent. "He was pretty feeble," Melanie snorted with derision. "Didn't last long."

Emerald started to tremble as her arm slid off the girl's shoulder and she hugged her arms round her own body, shivering.

Melanie looked appealingly at Tamsin. "I'm a good nurse! I know so much about how bodies work! I knew just where to press. It would look like a natural death. No-one would ever know!"

"And why did you attack Kevin Prenderghast?" Tamsin's arms were folded in front of her.

"He'd been staring over the heads of those women. I knew he'd clocked me outside the dining room just before that stupid woman started screaming. He may have seen me going in after Peter, or - or coming out! He had to go."

"But you messed that one up."

"I did. But I've given him a warning!" Her eyes shone even more brightly.

Tamsin shook her head slowly. Clearly bats, she thought to herself. "And you boasted to Martin about what you'd done?"

"I told him, yes, the next day. I told him he wouldn't have to worry any more about Threlgood finding him out. I thought he'd be so pleased!" She started to whimper again. "Relieved, you know. And now we had a secret between us. I'd be important to him .."

"And instead?"

"He pushed me away! He despised me." She clenched her fists. "He said he'd been young and stupid and drunk when he did what he did. That I was just a cold heartless cow and he wanted nothing more to do with me." She started to snivel. "He said they couldn't prove anything, about the army thing. He was quite safe. He wasn't even grateful."

"When did you give him that note?"

"Today! After ... after I left the Elgar statue. I ran to his office and put it through his door. Is that how you found me out?" She looked aghast, suddenly realising her stupidity.

Tamsin said, "My father always used to say, 'Men are like buses. Never run after one. There's always another one coming.'"

"But I don't know if another one will be coming for you, Melanie, not where you're going," said Emerald sadly.

Melanie rolled over and sprawled face down on the pavement, groaning.

"The only one coming for you at the moment is going to be wearing a police uniform," said Tamsin as she dialled 999 and put her phone to her ear.

## CHAPTER TWENTY-TWO

At this, Melanie crumpled and sobbed pathetically. She seemed to be seeing the reality of what she'd done at last. Emerald gave her a small pat on the shoulder and moved away silently.

Tamsin stood with Banjo, also silent. The chase had been exciting, but she could never take pleasure in "the kill". She rang Feargal and spoke quietly.

"Where are you? ... Well, can you turn round and come to the vet's? ... Yes, now. Got a scoop for you."

Feargal hadn't gone far from Malvern and arrived in time to see a blue and yellow police car, its lights flashing, pulling up. The commotion brought two other nurses and one of the vets out from the surgery, and they stood, mouths open, as the scene unfolded before them, Tamsin explaining to the policeman what had happened. The nurses clung to each other in the doorway. None of them seemed to want to speak to Melanie.

The burly Sergeant - who looked huge in all his police kit, his stab vest covered with walkie-talkies, tasers, batons, and goodness knows what else - nodded to Tamsin, then quickly trotted out his caution to the dejected nurse. "I am arresting you on suspicion of murder. You do not have to say anything but it may harm your defence if you do not mention when questioned something which you later rely on in court. Anything you do say may be given in evidence. Do you understand?" Melanie nodded without a word. He took her limp hands and snapped on the handcuffs, then asked in a softer voice, "Are you alright? Do you need medical assistance?" Melanie was now totally unresisting and shook her head hopelessly. He helped her up gently and led her to the back seat of his car. "You'll be taken to the station now."

Shutting the car door he turned back to Tamsin, "She's one of the two we've been keeping an eye on. There were conflicting statements. You beat us to it!" he laughed. "You'll need to come down to the station too, and tell us what you know, so we can prepare a case. But her confession should be sufficient. Think she'll stick to it?"

"I think she will. She seems broken."

"She's a nurse," said Emerald. "She must have been in anguish over what she'd done."

"Not anguished enough not to try it again," Feargal reminded her. The Sergeant looked quizzically at him.

"She pushed a man down the Elgar steps this morning. He was not badly hurt and didn't want to report it. He had no idea who'd done it."

"But she held up her hand for that one too," said Tamsin.

"He was there on the night of the murder," Emerald explained.

"It was Kevin Prenderghast," said Feargal.

"You can tell us all about that too. I think it would be a good idea if you all followed me down. The Custody Sergeant will be checking her in and she'll be questioned in the morning. But given the day that's in it, if you can tell us what you know tonight, you can enjoy your day tomorrow."

"You working tomorrow?" asked Feargal.

"No peace for the wicked!" he laughed, "good day for domestics and drunk driving." He headed back to his flashing car, the hunched shape of his prisoner just visible through the window. "That dog of yours is pretty useful," he laughed as he opened the driver's door. "We'll need to sign him up!"

So it was a good two hours later that a very tired Tamsin and her equally exhausted friends left the station.

"Want to come back with us, Feargal?"

"If you've got food, then .. is the Pope a Catholic?" he grinned.

"We keep a hoard of food just in case you visit, don't worry!" Emerald said, and they set off for Pippin Lane, where Tamsin rustled up some dinner while Emerald lighted the fire and fed the dogs and cat, with a special treat for Banjo the hero.

"We haven't actually got that much food, as we're both away over Christmas and the fridge is pretty bare. But don't panic, Feargal! We'll fill your hollow legs with something palatable!"

Tamsin tapped out a quick message to Charity:

*Melanie under arrest for murder. You may like to tell Dorothy tomorrow? I'll tell you more next week. Thanks for your insights! Merry Christmas.*

Then by tacit agreement they didn't talk any more about Peter Threlgood's murder while they ate. Instead they regaled each other with funny stories from past Christmases, Feargal and Emerald finding they shared a loathing for jigsaw puzzles. They played with the dogs, and Feargal instituted a new trick for Quiz. He handed her a pencil and said, "Take it to Em," whereupon Quiz went over to Emerald and sat smartly in front of her, holding the pencil in her soft mouth.

"Thank you Quiz," said Emerald as she took the pencil and gave the dog a morsel from her plate. "Look! She hasn't crunched it at all!" Emerald held the pencil up to show them. "Here, Quiz, take it to Mum."

Quiz took the pencil again and looked about in puzzlement. "She doesn't know who 'Mum' is," Tamsin smiled. "She only knows what you call me."

"Of course! Quiz - take it to Tamsin."

This time the dog understood and took the pencil to Tamsin, who took it with a "Thank you Quizzy," and a big hug for her special dog.

"There's something I still have to ask you," said Feargal apologetically after their game was over, and Quiz had returned his pencil to him intact. "What made you know it was Melanie? We were all looking at Martin and Steve."

"Two wise people-watchers - that's Molly and Charity - both saw what I had missed. That there was something between Martin and Melanie."

"Obviously, as it turns out, a much bigger something for Melanie than for Martin," Emerald stroked Opal, as ever on her lap, ruefully.

"And being in love can lead people down a very rocky road. Who knows what goes on in their minds. We knew Martin had not been near the dining room. And we were distracted by thinking about Steve too much."

"We were! Poor maligned fellow .." Feargal grinned.

"I think he'll survive," laughed Tamsin. "I'm sure he's weathered worse in his time. It just occurred to me this evening - remember when we visited the shop, Emerald? He was getting his ear chewed by his missus for smoking in the back office when he's meant to be giving up."

"Oh yes, I do remember! So perhaps .."

"Yes! He was outside having a smoke, as far away from Dottie as he could easily get on a busy day."

"As pure and innocent as the driven snow!" chortled Feargal.

"I was still considering him though, up till this afternoon. But it suddenly all became clear when I saw the note I told you about. It had to be Melanie!"

"Foolish of her, to leave that note. Clear evidence of her connection with Martin."

"Yeah, she was really crazy about him. Thought that murdering Peter would curry favour with him. Mad, on so many levels ..." Emerald sighed.

"There's one vestige of goodness that comes out of all this," said Tamsin. "When Jeremy's father comes up for the funeral - whenever that's to be - Dorothy can tell him that his son's death is solved, with no stain on his character. Who knows, he may want to pursue it with the new evidence. This man has caused him the loss of two of his family!"

"Directly or indirectly," said Emerald.

"You know, Martin Bramwell is pretty despicable," Feargal folded his arms. "I think when the police get all this information they may want to start proceedings against him - or at least pass it to the Ministry of Defence. He shouldn't get away with it."

"Well, it's all done and dusted for now! *We* can stop thinking about it, and let the authorities take over." Tamsin said, leaning over the dog on her lap to reach her coffee mug.

"And we can start thinking about visiting Susannah! Look at the time!" exclaimed Emerald.

"You're going visiting?" Feargal raised an enquiring eyebrow.

"Yes! Susannah's invited us over to see her latest crop of goatlets - she's just finished kidding."

"I'm sure you could come too, if you like. You remember Susannah from that business with the yogurt and scones?"

"Of course - lovely person. Will she mind if I just fetch up there?"

"No, I'm sure she won't. I got her a bottle of champagne to celebrate - well it's fizzy wine actually - can't quite run to real champagne," Tamsin grinned. "You can carry it in, Feargal, to be sure of your welcome!"

"Sounds good to me. What time are we due there?"

"Any time, but I think it needs to be soon. Susannah still has to be up early for milking whether it's Christmas Day or not." And so saying, she got up to let the dogs out to the garden while Feargal helped Emerald clear away the coffee things. Tamsin whizzed upstairs to fetch the bottle of fizz from her store room, and settled the dogs while they all wrapped themselves up in coats, hats, and gloves.

"Christmas presents for you tomorrow, my lovely dogs!" and she gave each one a kiss on the top of their head.

"Better take my car," said Feargal, "as there's three of us. I don't fancy riding in a dog crate!"

"And we don't want to fall out of favour with the good Chief Inspector Hawkins by carrying an illegal passenger!" added Tamsin.

And so they set off, up through the Wyche Cutting, the bright moonlight of the clear cold night casting an eerie glow over the fields and farms that came into view below them as they rounded the mighty Malvern Hills.

# CHAPTER TWENTY-THREE

They bounced along Susannah's potholed lane up the hill to her farm, which lay quiet in the moonlight.

"No goats to be seen?" said Feargal, craning his neck to look over the hedge.

"This is a goat hotel!" said Emerald. "They're all in warm strawy, hay-filled barns - just wait and see. They have every mod con a goat could wish for."

Susannah came out to greet them as they scrambled out of Feargal's car.

"We brought Feargal, hope you don't mind?"

"Of course not! The more the merrier," said Susannah with a broad smile. "Still keeping us abreast of the news at the *Malvern Mercury*, Feargal?"

"I do my best," he laughed, presenting the chunky bottle of sparkling wine.

"Ooh, come in and let's open this - I could do with a celebration. Thirteen kids!" She tossed the remark over her shoulder as she opened the kitchen door. "Three sets of twins, a large singleton, and two lots of triplets. And my best milkers are already breaking winter milk records for me."

They followed her into her warm kitchen, the Aga quietly pumping out heat in the corner.

"That's wonderful! You're kept busy with orders?"

"I am. You see, people don't understand that animals have seasons for kidding, and seasons for drying off. They want goats' milk and they want it now! So I've got to keep the supply going all year."

"Does it work out more expensive in the winter? Ooh, it's lovely and warm in here!" Emerald peeled off her mittens and stuffed them into her coat pockets, before unwinding her scarf and draping it on the back of a chair, along with the coat.

"Yes! A lot more - but it evens out. I've had to put the prices up anyway over the last few months. Hate doing that." Susannah pulled a face.

"You have to charge the right money!" protested Tamsin, "You work hard to provide all these goat products."

"You're right, of course," Susannah conceded.

"I'm so glad that bad business last summer didn't have a lasting effect," Tamsin gave Susannah a warm hug.

"Storm in a yogurt pot," Susannah grinned. "Thanks to you it all passed over very quickly." She gave each of them a small present tied with ribbon, then slid the kettle off the hotplate and fetched glasses for the wine.

"Ooh thank you Susannah!" said Emerald, untying the bow and sniffing her present. "My favourite soap! I love the geranium one."

Feargal was looking puzzled at his gift.

"It's soap made with goats' milk," Tamsin explained to him. "It's really good for your skin. Susannah makes it."

Feargal sniffed his present appreciatively, thanked Susannah warmly and slipped it into his pocket. Then he set about opening the bottle with the 'pop' that is always greeted with cries of delight - as it was this evening.

"Just a small one for me," he said, as their hostess poured. "I'm driving."

"You'd better have some of this Christmas cake then, to help sop it up." And she cut some slices of the rich fruit cake and passed everyone a plate.

"We're dying to see these little kids," said Tamsin, taking a big bite of the delicious cake. "Homemade marzipan!" she exclaimed. "What a treat. I don't know how you find the time to do so much," she shook her head in wonder as she munched.

"Full disclosure: I bought this from Hilda at the Farmers' Market," she grinned. "We'll go out to see the kids a bit later. I'll be checking them all before bed anyway. Some of them are still on their mothers for a few more days. But the rest are on four bottles a day, so I'll be feeding them too. Anyone want to volunteer for feeding duty?"

Two hands shot up, with cries of "Me, me!"

"What about you Feargal?"

"I've never done that - will you show me how?"

"Of course. It's easy enough as long as you make sure to tilt the bottle so they don't gulp air. Colic can be a killer for kids."

"I'm not sure I should, in that case."

"You can't weasel out of it that easily, young man! It'll be wonderful to have a helping hand."

Feargal touched his finger to his head in a salute. "Ok then, I'd love to."

"I've got a friend who saves hedgehogs," said Tamsin, munching her cake. "Sometimes he has to feed them milk with a dropper or a syringe, apparently, if they're very young."

"How lovely! Goat colostrum is excellent for orphaned baby animals, you know." Susannah saw the fog appear on Emerald's face and added quickly, "The first milk - *biestings* they call it. It's very thick and rich and yellowish. Then the milk comes pink for a while. We don't drink the milk for the first four days. Once it's chalk-white in colour it's ready for us. I always keep some biestings in the freezer, just in case."

"Thanks, I'll tell him! He may need some one day."

Emerald cast a thoughtful glance at her friend, then announced, "While you've been up to your ears in kids and col- colostrum? - Tamsin's been doing her stuff with Malvern's latest murder."

"That's why we're so late. We were tied up at the police station - I don't mean literally tied up!" Tamsin said quickly, with a laugh. "We weren't the ones in handcuffs."

"Another murder? I hadn't read about that," Susannah looked accusingly at Feargal.

"The police didn't want to release that information officially while they were working behind the scenes," replied Feargal. "There'll be plenty about it in Christmas week! I was drafting the article while I was waiting in the cop shop for my interview."

"I'm glad I missed it. Got enough on my plate! But it's all over now? The guilty cannot escape the fury of The Malvern Hills Detective," Susannah smiled.

"All over. It had one good outcome though - a very nice person whose old dog is ageing has acquired a new younger dog. That's got to be good! I'll tell you about it another time. Though Feargal's article will enlighten you, no doubt. Now we can sleep safely in our beds at night once more!"

"And enjoy a lovely, blameless, worry-free Christmas," said Emerald with a big sigh.

"I don't think mine will be that worry-free," chuckled Tamsin, "I'll be spending time protecting my dogs from the ravages of my nephew and nieces."

"They can always go in the van if it gets too raucous, can't they?" asked Feargal. "I can't imagine Banjo managing very well with a crowd of over-excited kids .. er, children," he smiled at Susannah.

"Banjo loves kids, doesn't he, Susannah. I mean, real kids!"

"He does! Give them a few weeks to get a bit bigger and you can bring him up to play with them again."

"Thanks! But children, not so much. He actually loves my Mum though, Feargal, and she's very protective of him. We'll manage," Tamsin smiled.

Emerald was attracted to a framed poem on the kitchen wall, and put down her glass to go over and look at it, resting her hand on the warm Aga. "Oh, 'The Oxen'! Thomas Hardy! We did that at school. It was the only thing of Hardy that I actually liked."

The others got up to join her, and Feargal read the poem out loud.

---

*Christmas Eve, and twelve of the clock.*
    *"Now they are all on their knees,"*
    *An elder said as we sat in a flock*
    *By the embers in hearthside ease.*

*We pictured the meek mild creatures where*
    *They dwelt in their strawy pen,*
    *Nor did it occur to one of us there*
    *To doubt they were kneeling then.*

*So fair a fancy few would weave*
    *In these years! Yet, I feel,*
    *If someone said on Christmas Eve,*
    *"Come; see the oxen kneel,*

*"In the lonely barton by yonder coomb*
    *Our childhood used to know,"*
    *I should go with him in the gloom,*
    *Hoping it might be so.*

---

They stood entranced, listening to his rather pleasant lilting rendition of the poem, with that slight touch of Irish which made his voice so attractive.

"What's the time now?" said Emerald suddenly.

Susannah looked at the old kitchen clock on the wall. "Just turning midnight,"

"Quick! We just have time to see them all kneeling!"

Susannah shook her head gently with a smile and said, "Get your coats on, it's nippy out there."

And they all processed outside, their breath coming out in clouds in the still moonlit night, to the shed housing the newest mothers and their kids. As the goats heard their footsteps crunching over the gravel there were a few quiet "Me-e-ehs". Susannah opened the big barn door and switched on a light, dim amidst its coat of cobwebs.

"They're kneeling!" exclaimed Emerald, quite awestruck.

"They are!" echoed Tamsin, mouth open.

"Now they're standing up," Feargal watched the nearest mother as she got to her feet.

Susannah, who knew well that goats get up from lying down by kneeling, smiled fondly at them.

"We saw them kneel!" Emerald couldn't get over it. *"Christmas Eve, and twelve of the clock. Now they are all on their knees."* Her eyes were wide, and a little misty.

Feargal had worked out what was going on, but he was captivated by Emerald's wonder, and wouldn't burst her bubble for anything.

As the mothers stood up, in the hope of a bucket of feed from their goat-keeper, the little newborn kids scrambled to their feet too, and ducked under their dam to latch on to her udder and suckle. The mothers bleated softly to them, and turned to nose their tails, which wagged from side to side very fast.

"You only hear goats talk like that when their kids are new-born," Susannah said quietly, not wanting to interrupt the moment.

They all stood quietly and relished what they were seeing in the gloomy, hay-scented, warm barn. The silence of the Christmas night. New life, mothers' love. Life goes on.

"Aah," said Tamsin. "What a wonderful Christmas present to the world!"

*If you enjoyed this story, I think you'll LOVE* **Game, Set, and Catch!** https://mybook.to/GameSetCatch - *the next book in the series, which finds Tamsin starting a new sport where all is not quite what it seems ...*

**Tamsin Kernick joins a quaint rural tennis club in sight of the Malvern Hills, only to discover that the drama on the court is nothing compared to the trouble brewing off it.**

When a member is found dead, Tamsin and her trusty canine companions must serve up some justice before someone else wins the match. As her friends from her favourite café rally to uncover the truth, Tamsin finds herself tangled in a net of secrets, lies, and deadly rivalries. Can she ace this mystery before it's too late?

Tamsin's super dogs are at the forefront of serving this criminal their just deserts (but not the luscious desserts from the café!). No ne'er-do-well is a match for these three dogs and their amazing tricks!

**For lovers of Agatha Christie and James Herriot, dogs, and the English countryside.**

To find out a little about how Tamsin arrived in Malvern and began Top Dogs, you can read this free amusing interview with Feargal for the Malvern Mercury:

https://books.lucyemblem.com/interview

Bonus? We'll be able to let you know when Tamsin's next adventure is ready for you!

And if you enjoyed this book, I'd love it if you could whiz over to where you bought it and leave a brief review, so others may find it and enjoy it as well, and be kind to their animals!

## ALL THE TAMSIN KERNICK COZY ENGLISH MYSTERIES

Where it all began ..
https://urlgeni.us/Lucyemblemcozy

Sit, Stay, Murder! *
https://mybook.to/SitStayMurder

Ready, Aim, Woof! *
https://mybook.to/ReadyAimWoof

Down Dog! *
https://mybook.to/downdog

Barks, Bikes, and Bodies! *
https://mybook.to/BarksBikesBodies

Ma-ah, Ma-ah, Murder!
https://mybook.to/MaahMaahMurder

Snapped and Framed!
https://mybook.to/SnappedFramed

Christmas Carols and Canine Capers! A Howling Good Christmas Mystery!
https://mybook.to/Christmascozy

Game, Set, and Catch!
https://mybook.to/GameSetCatch

\* Also available in Large Print

https://mybook.to/TamsinKernickCozies

## ABOUT THE AUTHOR

From an early age I loved animals. From doing "showjumping" in the back garden with Simon, the long-suffering family pet - many years before Dog Agility was invented - I worked in the creative arts till I came back to my first love and qualified as a dog trainer.

Working for years with thousands of dogs and their colourful owners - from every walk of life - I found that their fancies and foibles, their doings and their undoings, served to inspire this series of cozy mysteries.

While the varying characters weave their way through the books, some becoming established personnel in the stories, the stars of the show are the animals!

They don't have human powers. They don't need to. They have plenty of powers of their own, which need only patience and kindness to bring out and enjoy with them.

If you enjoyed this story, I would LOVE it if you could hop over to where you purchased your book and leave a brief review!

Lucy Emblem